CEDAR VALLEY

CEDAR VALLEY

NEVADA CARTER

A Black Horse Western

ROBERT HALE · LONDON

© Nevada Carter 1993
First published in Great Britain 1993

ISBN 0 7090 5146 8

Robert Hale Limited
Clerkenwell House
Clerkenwell Green
London EC1R 0HT

Photoset in North Wales by
Derek Doyle & Associates, Mold, Clwyd.
Printed and bound in Great Britain by
WBC Ltd, Bridgend, Mid-Glamorgan.

1

A Minor Mystery

Rangemen like Mountain Men learned by experience: Flat, open country meant wind, scrub-brush country meant little water, anywhere mountains rose so high a man had to tilt his head to see their rims, meant cold winters and heavy snows, juniper trees, which after a rain smelled like wet diapers and cedar trees meant long droughts but, unlike junipers which indicated poor soil, cedars grew where there was deep soil, probably because roots had to go far down for moisture.

Pine trees grew profusely at lower elevations in country with moisture. Fir trees only grew at higher elevations often in rocky country where there was a good melt in spring.

The country around Cedarton had them all, but not many junipers. The soil was deep, water like veins ran in many places. One particular wild creek had been diverted to provide water for the ditches on both sides of town.

That had happened maybe fifteen years earlier

when Cedarton hadn't had a name; it was called Buffalo Wallow, but the bison had been disappearing even then. Now, there hadn't been a buffalo in the Cedarton country for years, although the wallows were still around, fairly deep places in the ground where large animals had got down to roll and wallow in clouds of dust, and those places would still be visible half a century later.

There were high mountains but many miles distant from the town, which was in the centre of a huge, rolling meadow of tall grass. Those far-away mountains had rough peaks, several of the higher ones with ice year round, which made summers pleasant, particularly if the wind blew from the north over those ice fields.

Cedar Valley itself was wider than it was long. Miles of good stock country with grass stirrup high, something which would be less tall as years passed, a reduction which was so slight it would be two generations before stockmen realised the reason they had to graze farther each season because over-grazing had inexorably depleted their range.

The town was sturdy with a very wide main thoroughfare. It had shade trees. Very few of the original cedars which had marked the area earlier still stood, but other varieties of trees flourished including an apple tree in almost every yard, along with imported sycamores lining both sides of Main Street.

Cedarton had very few vestiges of its early days, even the log buildings had been sided-over with planed lumber, but there were folks around town who remembered how things had been.

Stories of Indian attacks could be vividly recalled at the drop of a hat. As Link Mallow the pool hall proprietor, himself an old timer, had often said, after ten or fifteen years even folks who had survived those battles couldn't recognise them as they were now related.

Lincoln Mallow, named for a President who had still been alive when Link had been born, was a grey, eagle-eyed, man who had to be in his late sixties but who acted and thought more like a man in his forties, took particular delight in deriding some of those hair-raising stories. It got so old-timers avoided Link, except for a few like-minded old gaffers who had also lived through perilous times and dangerous events. This small band of Cedarton's citizens were considered by some of the male late-comers and all of the female late-comers as uncouth, ribald, cantankerous old screwts who didn't know civilised men shaved daily or at least trimmed their beards, and who wouldn't have been caught dead in greasy old buckskin shirts.

It was not a noticeable division of citizenry. In fact Isaac Bowen the local constable – called 'sheriff' by just about everyone because, although his jurisdiction as town constable was limited to Cedarton he was the only law in Cedar Valley, ignored the distinction when he could, and when he couldn't he simply laughed about it.

Isaac was a good-natured man, not handsome but not ugly either. He was young by local standards, about thirty, and he was rawboned, ham-fisted and fearless.

Autumn came with its customary precursors; turning leaves, brisk mornings, snow caps on the distant peaks, and dust-raising long cattle drives toward a distant siding where great networks of corrals had been built by the railroad people to accommodate herds destined for such places as Kansas City or Chicago.

Cedar Valley cattle drives each autumn were identical to drives through the cattle country. It was a long time between paydays for cowmen who only made a gather and drive once a year, so the predominant hope as drovers passed Cedarton, was that beef prices might be high.

Good or bad, there was profit; free grass, good weather and limited predator-loss ensured a profit, what live-stockmen had to gamble on was how *much* profit. This made the difference between new saddles and harness, perhaps an elegant buggy, furniture and other incidentals, and putting such ideas off for another year.

Neil Garfield had been making the drive since his early teens and he was now grey as a badger, weathered, lined and less likely to make snap judgements or shoot off his mouth than he had been in earlier years.

Neil had a wife and two daughters. In angry exasperation he had named his second-born Neil. He knew it was a girl but he'd wanted a son too badly to yield.

No one thought it strange to give a girl a boy's name. There were some very unique names hung onto babies west of the Missouri River.

Garfield and the constable were old friends. On

the return trip from the fall drive Neil sent his riders on ahead to the ranch while he stopped in town, cut the dust from his gullet at the saloon, then sauntered down to the jailhouse to learn if anything worth knowing had happened in his absence.

Not much had happened, Ike Bowen told the stockman over a cup of hot java. Ike sat at his desk half smiling. 'With you'n everyone else driving south there hasn't been a drunk rangeman in here in over a month.'

The cowman smiled. 'They'll be along. It was a long drive with no stops except in camp.'

'How was the market?' Constable Bowen asked.

Neil Garfield sighed and leaned holding his coffee cup. 'I figured somethin' out on the ride back, Ike. Did you ever hear of someone gettin' scalped an' kept their hair? Those damned cattle buyers can do that an' stockmen got no choice. They stick together like peas in a pod. I must have talked to five, six of them. Every blessed one offered the same price. It wasn't low, mind you, an' it wasn't as high as I've seen it. We'll do all right. It's just the way those highbinders is organised so's us cowmen can take it or leave it.'

Garfield smiled. 'Someday I'll quit, move into town an' buy a business where a man can stay warm in winter an' cool in summer.'

The constable laughed. 'You'll die complainin' about cattle prices and makin' drives, Neil.'

Garfield unwound up out of his chair, dropped a dilapidated old hat on his head, winked and walked out where his horse was waiting.

Constable Bowen finished his coffee, made a casual round of town, ended up at the pool hall where Link Mallow was using a little brush to smooth the velvet on his three tables. Link looked up. 'I saw Mister Garfield pass a while back. That'll mean they're all back.' Link straightened up. 'I'll like havin' some trade for a change. Since that mule-ridin' Bible banger come to town first of the month business dropped off to beat hell. Ike, do you expect you could get the Town Council to make an ordinance against travellin' preachers?'

The constable sank into a chair shaking his head. 'Link, you get lots of trade in winter. The town papas wouldn't even think of banning preachers. If they did an' their wives found out about it –'

'That's part of the trouble with this world, Ike. Too many womenfolks speakin' their minds. When I was young –'

The constable's laughter interrupted the older man, who squinted. 'You think it's funny? They's a bad influence, Ike. Look how close they come to forcin' the saloon to be closed on Sunday.' Link also sat down holding his little brush in a gnarled fist. 'Month or so back I read in a newspaper where some danged woman went around town with a hatchet chopping down bars. You know where that kind of thing can end? Ike, I tell you it'll get out of hand. Next thing you know they'll be callin' for us to give them the vote.'

Bowen ambled up to the north end of town, which had a stage company corralyard on the west side, and an old converted army barracks on the east side, now known as the Cedartown Hotel. Up there he heard a ruckus coming from the corralyard, but by the time he got down there the fractious harness horse had been subdued.

The head Indian saw Ike out front and walked toward him shaking his head. 'One damned rock an' you'd think that horse had been hit by a cannonball.'

Ike was puzzled. 'A rock? Someone in the yard hit him with a rock?'

'No, it was west of town. The driver didn't stop to look. Someone hit the horse in the side with a good-sized rock. It's swole, maybe a rib's cracked, but that's no call for the blasted animal to throw a fit. I had him put in a corral by hisself an' fed good. For a fact if he's got a cracked rib we can't put him in harness for quite a while.'

Ike leaned on the palisaded wall. 'Where did someone hit the horse?'

'West about a mile before you come to the southward bend heading for town.' The corralyard man made a wide gesture, palms up. 'Why, I got no idea. No one was around, there wasn't no attempt to stop the coach. Just that big rock comin' out of some trees to hit that horse smack-dab in the side.'

Ike knew the area where this had happened. The nearest set of buildings was about another mile west of where the incident had occurred. That was the Garfield outfit. The Garfields had two daughters, both well grown. Throwing rocks was something boys did. There were no buildings closer than several miles beyond the Garfield place, and although those folks out yonder had sons, they were full grown.

Ike said, 'That stand of cedars beside the road

where that big rock is?'

The stage company's man nodded. 'Damned kids, Sheriff.'

'The driver didn't see anyone?'

'No, but there's that big rock an' the trees.'

Ike continued to lean. It did not make sense to stone a stage for no apparent reason. Nor could he imagine for the life of him why someone would do such a senseless thing.

He and the corralyard boss walked back to the round pole corral where a stocky bay horse was lipping up stalks from the ground.

The lump was the size of an apple. Ike said, 'Cracked rib sure as hell. Maybe broken.' He faced his companion. 'Those trees are a fair distance from the road, Lewis. Whoever threw that rock must have had one hell of an arm for the rock to still have that kind of power when it hit the horse.'

The corralyard boss nodded, clearly having other things to do; besides, the horse could have all the time needed to recover. As far as he was concerned, unfathomable mystery or not, it was over with and there had been no serious injury.

He turned when someone called, nodded to the constable and hiked back toward the front of the yard where his office was located.

Constable Bowen leaned a long time studying the horse, who seemed to suffer only when he walked; otherwise, when he stood still he showed no indication of pain.

Ike went back to the jailhouse after an early dinner at the cafe. It was a mystery and he had never like mysteries. By making a guess he arrived at the conclusion that whoever had hurled that rock, if he was out of sight among the trees by the big boulder he had to have a hurling ability the likes of which Isaac Bowen had never heard of.

Then too there was the reason why someone had thrown the rock. The mystery here was not just why, but also the reason he had not followed up. If he had been a highwayman ... but that didn't make sense. Highwaymen used guns, not stones, and they stopped stages, they didn't just hide and hurl stones as the vehicles passed.

There had been no damage. In fact as it turned out, none of the three passengers inside the coach even knew the rock had been thrown.

He went in search of the driver, but he was already on his way south on a new schedule and the corralyard boss sounded almost annoyed when he said, 'It's nothing, Ike. Some silly idiot ... The horse'll be all right in a few weeks, no one was hurt.'

The constable nodded about all that and said he'd like to talk to the whip when he returned. The corralyard boss agreed to that, nodded and walked away. In his opinion the constable was nit-picking, life was full of silly idiots going around annoying folks.

Maybe he was right. He probably was, but Isaac Bowen was like the proverbial dog who would not give up a bone.

Fortunately, as it turned out.

2

Some Thoughts

The shock brought the entire community to a standstill. Nothing like it had happened in thirty years. There were rustlers, horsethieves, even an occasional robber in town, but the story Neil Garfield's rider brought to Cedarton stopped folks in their tracks.

Garfield had returned home to find his riders gone on a vengeance trail leaving just one man at the ranch. There was little he could do, he was a cowhand, but he did the best he could.

Garfield's wife and daughter were dead. His remaining daughter, the tom-boy named after her father had taken a carbine and a six-gun to the loft with her. The raiders left in a swirl of dust as abruptly as they had appeared. They peppered the front of the barn but Garfield's surviving daughter had fought back until the marauders ran for it, heading northwest, not chased away by the girl in the loft; their kind did not frighten, but neither did they linger after two brutal murders and a wild ransacking of the house.

By the time Isaac Bowen heard the story it was late evening. He had been up yonder trying to figure something out about that rock-hurling incident. He returned to town no wiser than when he had left to be told the grisly story of the murders and plundering which had left Neil Garfield a widower with one surviving daughter.

It was too late to ride out there, darkness came swiftly in Wyoming's high country, even in early summer, but the following morning he rode to the Garfield yard, was met by the solitary rangeman who told him Mister Garfield had saddled his favourite seal-brown horse without saying where he was going, and the cowboy had not seen him since, nor had the other riders returned from their manhunt.

The rider showed Bowen the house. It looked like a herd of wild horses had run through it. He also showed Ike the pair of shrouded bodies lying side by side on a bed in the back of the house.

Ike wandered. The raid had been fierce and savage. Neil's wife had been shot in the back. His dead daughter had powder scorch on her blouse, she had been killed by someone standing very close when he fired.

Drawers had been pulled out, contents spilled, pawed through, cupboards had been swept clean by hurrying hands and arms. Even the bedding had been slashed and torn. Here, Ike stood a while; outlaws did not slash mattresses unless they were seeking valuables, money, perhaps jewels.

He returned to the yard, but shod-horse tracks

were everywhere. The rangerider said he and the others figured there had been five of them. He gestured somewhat vaguely. 'They went sort of on an angling run northeast.' The rider dropped his arm. 'We figure they struck the day before we got back … Sheriff, to my way of thinkin' – do you reckon they knew only the womenfolk was here? An' if they did do you expect they knew we was gone, maybe from watchin' the yard, or maybe … someone in our area who would know about the drive?'

Ike leaned in pleasant sunshine out front of the barn where he lighted a thin, dark cigar. The rider sat on a bench. 'If Mister Garfield catches 'em, I sure wouldn't want to be in their boots. You know him pretty well, do you, Sheriff?'

'Pretty well.'

'Well, he'll make them bastards die for five hours, I can tell you that.'

Ike removed the cigar and regarded the rangeman as he said, 'Only five hours? Well … tell him I was here.'

The rider watched Constable Bowen ride back the way he had come, it was mid-afternoon. The rider climbed to the loft and squinted out the mow-door. There was no sign of either Mister Garfield or the other riders. Around him was a litter of brass casings. He climbed back down and spun with hair rising when he heard a sound near the front barn opening.

It was Neil, standing loosely, expressionless. 'What did he want?' she asked.

The rider told of taking the constable through

the house, of their minimal discussion, then he said, 'Why didn't you show up?'

The tall, muscular woman turned her back without replying. She had rusty-red hair, was tall, angular, noticeably a female but just barely. She could ride and rope with the best men in the area. She wasn't pretty, but she had a distinctive magnetism and a good sense of humour, but not today.

Still with her back to the rider she said, 'He can't do anything. It was two days ago. The way they rode, even with a relay of horses our riders can't catch them. Two days – they can be out of the valley by now.' She faced around, eyes flat, lips pulled down. 'I saw two of them plain as day … If it ever comes to that.'

She left the rider in the barn opening watching her stride toward the devastated main-house. He, like most men including her father had never quite understood the female Neil Garfield. She was liked by the riders, who teased her, which she laughed about, and upon the extremely rare occasions when she wore a dress, gussied up her face and put a ribbon in her hair, except that they knew what she was *really* like, they might have cottoned to her as a female woman. When she was dressed like that they called her Nell, not Neil.

She spent a miserable late evening alone at the ruined main-house with her sister and mother cold and shrouded in the back of the house. Her room had been wrecked, two chairs were deliberately smashed, her dresser drawers had been flung aside, the contents scattered, even her redwood-burl box of very private things had been rifled through and flung aside. She had stood in the doorway just looking, touching nothing, just looking. Her silver comb was broken where an indifferent boot had come down upon it. The tin-type photograph of her mother and father when they had been young, was scratched beyond repair, even her tomboy treasures such as a Barlow clasp knife she'd received on Christmas years ago, and some ribbons, a pair of ox-shoes and some arrowpoints, had been flung on the floor.

Isaac bowen had wondered when she had not appeared while he was in the yard. He had not asked the rangeman. He wondered if she hadn't gone manhunting with her father but doubted it; the rangeman would have mentioned it if she had.

By the time dusk was settling there was a subdued atmosphere at the cafe, at Link Mallow's pool hall, at the saloon south of the gunsmith's shop on the east side of the roadway.

Even the old-timers who had survived an era when such raids were not uncommon, were shocked; it had been almost half a lifetime since anything like it had happened in Cedar Valley.

As the shock wore off there was anger; men rode in all directions armed to the gills, but after the second day with no results manhunting dwindled. It was two days later that Neil Garfield rode into town looking drawn, beard-stubbled, older, as though he had aged overnight, and unap-proachable.

He tied up in front of the jailhouse, walked in beating off dust with his hat, nodded to Constable Bowen and folded down into a chair. 'They're still lookin',' he dully said. 'If it's the last thing I ever do, I want to find them.'

Ike spoke softly. 'Tracks, Neil?'

'They was like wolves, they rode hard, scattered now an' then before clubbin' together again … Northeast some distance before they halted in some trees. They rested their animals for an hour or two … Gawd what I wouldn't give to have been among them trees when they come along.' The dull eyes moved slowly to the constable's face. The older man straightened in his chair and leaned as though to arise. 'Nell saw two of 'em real good. I'll send her in so's she can look at your wanted dodgers, but it'll be a while, Sheriff; she don't want to see anyone.'

Garfield arose. 'We'll do the buryin' tomorrow. Private – but I'd take it kindly if you'd ride out, Ike. M'wife always set a lot of store by you.'

After the cowman departed Ike made a round of town; he had to shy away from questions by people who had seen Garfield tie up out front of the jailhouse.

He was passing the pool hall when Link Mallow spoke from his doorway. 'You need posse riders, Ike?'

'Mister Garfield's riders are after them.'

Ike nodded and strode down as far as the saloon. The proprietor was a stork of a man, long-legged, not one extra ounce of meat on his bones, with a knife scar along the slant of his jaw on the left side. His name was Jered Salte; all his life he had been saying 'with an e on the end'.

He was the antithesis of a saloonman, he spoke

when spoken to, never smiled, had endless patience when someone got to reminiscing, and was rumoured to have been a holy-terror of an outlaw years earlier up in Montana.

It could have been true, he certainly had characteristics folks associated with outlaws, but Jered Salte and Constable Bowen had been friends for years. When Ike walked in the saloon had only a sprinkling of customers. Jered leaned down on his bar, fixed the constable with his expressionless gaze and said, 'Two days' start ain't too much when the ground's soft, Isaac.'

Ike asked for a jolt. While the tall man went after it, the constable gazed around. Every face in the saloon was known to him. When Jered returned with the sticky glass he said, 'A good tracker could find them, no matter how much of a lead they got.'

Ike placed coins atop the bar as he agreed. 'We don't have any trackers that good, Jered. Mister Garfield's riders are after them.'

The saloonman said no more for a while. He leaned off the bar with both long arms crossed over his chest.

Bowen downed his jolt, sighed and leaned against the bar eyeing the tall man. 'Mister Garfield's girl saw two of them. He's goin' to send her to town to look at my dodgers. If she can recognise two, that'll lead to the others.'

Jered made a slow up and down motion with his head. 'Tell me somethin', Isaac. How many men do you know ever been captured off wanted dodgers.'

Ike answered truthfully. 'One. Twelve years ago. He didn't have sense enough to get rid of his beard. In fact he'd been born with one foot out of the stirrup. He wasn't really an idiot but awful close. I walked up on him by his supper fire, out in open country where a man could see his fire for five miles. Walked up, threw down and brought him in snivellin' about how every hand was set against him ... That's the only one, Jered.'

'I used to be pretty good at trackin', Isaac,' the expressionless tall man quietly said. 'How many was there?'

'Five.'

'Well hell, no matter how big a lead they got, five men ridin' in a group leave sign. It'd take a lot of ridin' but it could be done ... Isaac?'

The constable cocked his head slightly. 'Are you tellin' me you want to go manhunting?'

The stork-built man was quiet for a time. 'No, but there are times ... What they did wouldn't even set well with genuine outlaws ... Isaac; when's Mister Garfield's girl comin' to look at your posters?'

'I don't know. Why?'

'If you're goin' after them lads the sooner the better. She don't have to ride in tomorrow. In fact if they left good tracks she don't have to show up at all. Isaac, every day them bastards ain't caught increases the amount of ridin' their pursuers have to do.'

Constable Bowen returned to his jailhouse puzzling over what the very tall barman had said. The next morning after sunup he rigged out and headed for the Garfield yard. Fortunately the only matching coat and pants he owned were black.

They had a buckboard already hitched to a pair of light harness horses out front of the house when Ike rode in. No one greeted him. He cared for his horse in the barn, dusted off very carefully then crossed in the direction of the wagon where Garfield, his daughter, that rangeman Ike had spoken to when they had been alone in the yard, along with three other rangemen, Garfield riders, bronzed, lean men with freshly axle-greased boots, and solemn faces waited.

Without a word the men trouped inside behind Garfield, returned with the shrouded corpses, placed them gently on the wagon slats, and walked to the ranch graveyard beside the wagon. Garfield and his daughter rode.

The graves were waiting. Each body was placed on an edge of two graves. Mister Garfield read a prayer from The Good Book in a grimly controlled voice, pocketed the Book and leaned to assist lowering the bodies. It was very quiet.

Garfield's leggy daughter stood like a statue. Like her father she had iron control. Handfuls of soil were dropped into each grave, Garfield said a short prayer from memory before taking his daughter to the rig, handing her up, climbing in beside her and turning back the way they had come.

Ike folded his coat, put it and his hat aside, picked up a shovel and went to work with the others. Not a word was said until the graves had been filled and properly mounded, then a lined, leathery-hided man with thick, calloused hands leaned on his shovel looking at the constable.

'They run northeast,' he said. 'We shagged them to some trees near a big rock close by the roadway. Seemed they stopped there a spell then crossed the road and went straight as an arrow toward the mountains.

'We had to stop when it got dark. The last tracks went into some foothills. They still had to cross maybe five miles to reach the mountains, an' they never changed course even a little bit.' The rangeman paused to shift his stand with the shovel. 'We made a cold camp, picked up the sign the next mornin' an' kept on it until we couldn't go no further because the tracks petered across a big rock field.'

When the man stopped talking he looked at his companions, none of them looked back, but the constable did. 'Do you know them mountains?' he asked, every one of the rangemen shook his head.

Ike said, 'I do, most of the way to the top anyway. I've buck hunted up there every autumn since I been in this country … I'll tell you, gents, they can't cross over the rims an' go down the other side. It's solid ice for miles up there. Even with spiked shoes they'd have to be crazy to try it.'

The leathery-hided man with perpetually squinted eyes said, 'They're still up in there?'

'Likely not. They'd go east or west. I can't imagine them making a camp up in there. They sure as hell know by now the country's all stirred up.'

Another rider had a question: 'Why would they go up in there unless they had a good reason? All they had to do was turn off east or west an' have fairly level country with trees now'n then to pass over. It'd be a heap easier on their horses than goin' up into the mountains.'

With the sun descending they walked back to the yard, sweaty, tired and hungry. Ike went as far as the barn where he got his horse, nodded around and headed back for Cedarton.

Another damn mystery. He would have to make up a light pack and scour the mountains. Fortunately, he knew where every watercourse ran, where every meadow with decent horse feed was, but there was one hell of a lot of country up there.

There was also an excellent possibility that the renegades had rested their animals and were already moving farther away in one way or another.

The problem for Constable Bowen was – which way, east or west? Two men could ascertain which way they had gone a lot easier than one man could.

He arrived back in town at dusk, changed back into his everyday attire and went to the cafe for a meal, sat a while in the jailhouse often with bugs circling his overhead lamp, smoked a stogie, made his decision, blew out the lamp, locked up from outside and went up to the saloon, which had its normal complement, got a bottle and glass, took them to an empty table and sat down to wait.

Some nights the saloon did not have more than half a dozen or so customers. Some nights, like this one, it seemed everyone but the old gaffers were at the saloon.

It was a long wait, but Isaac Bowen did not mind, he was fed, had some popskull for company, and had a damned riddle that wouldn't have allowed him to sleep if he'd gone home to bed.

Jered Salte was as tall as Abe Lincoln was reputed to have been, maybe even taller. He lacked a little of looking starved but on the other hand he did not carry the kind of weight a man almost six and a half feet tall should carry.

He left the bar when only four or five customers were still leaning there, came to Ike's table with an old sour rag tucked into his waistband, sat down without speaking, nodding or smiling and considered the man opposite him.

Ike leaned to push the bottle and little glass forward. Jered ignored them. He did occasionally drink, but not often and never very much. He leaned bony too-long arms on the table, still silent.

'Seems the Garfield riders trailed them into the mountains,' Isaac stated.

'And …'

'And – lost the sign so they came back.'

Jered leaned back off the table gravely regarding the constable. 'There's no way they could go over the top.'

'No.'

'Well, it's been four days now.'

'Yep.'

Jered rubbed the tip of his nose. 'You're sure windy tonight.'

Ike almost grinned. 'They lost the sign over a rock field.'

Jered Salte considered that. 'Sheriff, I never yet knew a rangeman who could track a fat cow through a mud hole.'

Ike nodded agreeably. 'Have you ever known a saloonman who could do any better?'

Jered's eyes narrowed perceptibly. 'For the first time I'm thinkin' all these years I've underestimated you.'

'Is that a fact?'

'Yes sir. Are you leadin' up to something?'

'Would you be interested if I said I was?'

The saloonman's unwavering gaze assumed an expression of almost hard amusement. 'I told you the other night. It can be done. Lots of time's been lost so it won't be no picnic, but it can be done.'

'Who'll mind the saloon while you're gone?'

'I'll lock up; they can wait. Who'll mind the jailhouse?'

'The same. I'll lock it up. If someone gets into trouble before we get back, they can tie him to a tree.'

'Before sunrise in the morning, Sheriff. We got one hell of a long way before we even reach the foothills.'

Ike said, 'If it's goin' to be that long a hunt we better carry whatever we'll need.'

The saloonman arose as he said, 'That was real clever, Sheriff. How did you ever figure that out?'

Ike looked up. 'You better be the best sign reader south of Montana.'

Jered nodded. '*Including* Montana. See you before sunrise.'

3

The First Contact – a Lame Mare

It was darker than the inside of a boot when they left Cedarton riding by the stars up the coach road until they angled over open country westerly toward the mountains.

Twice they were startled. Once by a big dog wolf gorging on a dead calf. The second time was when a rodent-hunting owl who was concentrating on the ground came within five feet of flying into them. At the very last moment the bird sagged westerly and beat his wings with all the power he had.

Otherwise the ride, while cold, was uneventful. Where they passed the foothills, which were a distinct distance from high country, Isaac thought dawn was not far off.

Neither of them had said much since leaving town. There was not much to talk about; they were on a trail, or shortly would be; when they found

27

sign there would be something to talk about.

They had to zigzag quite a distance before locating shod-horse tracks on top of earlier shod-horse tracks. Here, they halted. 'That'll be Garfield's riders overlying the other sign,' Ike stated, and got an almost pained look from his companion, but no comment for a while. Not until Jered had read everything off the ground it was possible to make out in timbered darkness. Then all he said was, 'I think we got a horse goin' lame, Sheriff.'

He did not explain, but Jered Salte had never been a loquacious individual, something folks had noted in Cedarton long ago.

With dawn breaking everywhere except in the ancient forest, there was weak light. Not until the sun had climbed did patches of daylight streak through the timber, and by then Jered guessed about where the renegades had stopped to blow their animals. He made haste from here on, gambling that he was right. He was. They came around a field of enormous pock-marked prehistoric rocks, their horses smelled water, Jered un-shipped his carbine, held it across his lap and did not look down. He could have done this by tracking, but even imprints of shod horses over deep layers of pine and fir needles, while readable, required slow progress. Jered's idea, based partly on knowledge of this area and partly on a conviction that wherever the outlaws halted there had to be water, allowed him to come around the enormous stones into a tiny grassy clearing with a creek on its far side.

He sat, left hand with the reins, right hand holding the saddlegun in his lap, motionless and soundless for a long while. It was here, finally, that the constable's earlier strong suspicion was confirmed.

Jered Salte had not always been a saloon-keeper.

They dismounted; Ike remained with the horses while Jered prowled the area of the abandoned camp. Daylight reached through treetops into the little meadow. He put Ike in mind of an Indian the way he walked, halted, studied the ground, shifted his course to different areas and finally returned to lean down on his Winchester as he spoke.

'Five, for a fact. One's ridin' a steeldust-coloured animal. The feller with the tired critter that scuffs one foot like it's goin' lame, is riding a mare.' Jered gestured. 'East.' He dropped his arm and perceptibly wagged his head. 'Damn fools. They're skirtin' easterly holding to timber. If they'd used their heads they could have rode easterly down in flat country. Hell, they had a long head-start. They didn't have to wear their animals down climbin' this far up.'

The constable said nothing, but his thoughts were uncharitable; he had yet to encounter a really *coyote* outlaw; deadly ones, yes, vicious ones and merciless ones, yes, but smart ones – no.

They rested the animals then struck out on the easily defined trail hugging easterly around the massive thigh of a miles' long curving slope, which was actually not very hard on their animals.

They moved through an ancient forest which, in places, had trees almost as thick and close as the hair on a dog's back.

When the sun was high they halted beside the tracks to eat and speculate. Jered was of the opinion that the marauders had an objective somewhere ahead and, being a hard-headed and cynical realist, he gave it as his opinion that the outlaw band was heading for some isolated ranch or small village.

Isaac went through his memory of the easterly territory trying to remember locations which could be raided. There were cow outfits, hell there were isolated cow outfits throughout even the farthest environs of Cedar Valley, but exact locations were blurry in his mind.

Before leaving this rest-stop, Jered wiped his lips before saying, 'The feller on the mare is losin' headway. Not much, an' maybe his friends ain't noticed, but the mare's scuffing her sore leg a little more all the time.'

He looked straight at the constable. 'Sheriff, we're goin' to get this one.'

Isaac would have liked a cigar, but aside from the tinder condition of the highlands, the scent of strong smoke of any kind carried one hell of a distance, and while their prey had to be at least one day, more likely two days, ahead, the risk was not worth it.

Jered had an advantage, he chewed.

They rode until late afternoon with both of them becoming increasingly convinced the marauders had a destination; for one thing they did not deviate from their easterly course, for another thing they eventually began to make a more leisurely ride the way outlaws would do if they no longer worried about being caught from behind, and were taking their time about when and how to arrive at their next raid.

Jered said, 'It's most likely already happened, Sheriff. We're a long way behind them.'

Isaac had been thinking the same thing for half a day, but until the timber thinned out in late afternoon the smoke he watched for was not visible. After there was less timber he still saw no smoke.

But they hadn't fired the Garfield place; maybe burning raided places was not something they did, although for a fact raiders usually did set fires.

Jered had the probable answer. 'Smoke can be seen for a hell of a distance. Folks come to fires like steel to magnets. If these men don't set fires my guess is that it's because they don't want no smoke to give away what they're doin', which is raiding one isolated cow outfit after the other.' Jered paused to spray amber. 'Sheriff, I don't spend much time guessin' but these men got to know the country. They can't ride no deliberate trail unless they do … Let's get on with it.'

They halted where timber thickened again. The sun was still up there, but on its slanting-away course which allowed little light to reach through.

Ike was tired when they finally off-saddled by a brawling little white-water creek whose water was so cold it hurt a man's teeth.

It was a cold camp; they made no fire, but the grub they'd brought along went down just as well cold as hot. This time as they leaned against up-ended saddles, Ike fired up a stogie. There was not a breath of air stirring.

As Jered got comfortable he said, 'We'll get the one with the wore-down mare. Maybe tomorrow. By my calculations she's travellin' on guts, but the most iron-willed critter on earth gives out some time.'

Ike spoke while tipping ash. 'If they take him up behind one of them that'll slow down the whole bunch.'

Jered got rid of his cud, rinsed his mouth and drank briefly from the creek. As he eased down he said, 'Tell me somethin', Sheriff. Do you figure there must be a better way to make a living?'

'Better than what, Jered?'

'Raidin' ranches, robbin' stages, blowin' open bank safes.'

'And murderin' womenfolk in cold blood?'

'I never knew men who'd do that.'

'But you've known the other kind?'

'... How long have we known each other, Sheriff?'

'Must be six or seven years. Why?'

'That ain't long enough for you to ask personal questions ... Wake me up in an hour.'

Ike smiled at the scimitar moon. He was more weary than sleepy, for although he did his share of saddlebacking during the course of doing his job, it had been quite a spell since he'd been on one of these unrelenting, wearing-down manhunts. They sapped a man for a fact.

He wondered about Neil and his surviving daughter. By now they had heard in town that the constable and the saloonman were gone. It wouldn't be hard to surmise *why* they were gone. He also wondered about the men up ahead somewhere; had they raided and murdered again? If he accepted Jered's notion, he should worry about what they would find maybe before tomorrow night.

He rapped the beanpole of a man on the bottoms of his boots. Jered awoke and sat up. He had been a very light sleeper for years. They rigged out and were back on the trail within a half hour – and encountered something they'd run into earlier; it was difficult even for a very good sign-reader to follow tracks in semi-darkness over springy layers of needles that popped back up after being trod on.

One factor helped Jered; there were five sets of shod-horse tracks. He did occasionally swing off to lead his horse because he could make out faint indentations better on foot than from the saddle. At night anyway.

Jered growled from up ahead. 'I hope those bastards is as tired as I am. If they'd kill a little time we could get a tad closer.'

Ike agreed. 'It'll be like the dead fighting the dead if we got to keep this up.'

Jered's next remark made his intention very clear. 'Fight hell. Five to one odds ain't a fight, Sheriff, it's a massacre. We're goin' to skulk up onto them.'

Isaac looped his reins, fished forth a cigar, cut the tip off with his clasp knife and cheeked it the way Jered pouched his cud.

Pure tobacco was a lot different from molasses-cured tobacco. He spat the leaves out, saw Jered looking back and shrugged. Jered spoke from a perfectly straight face. 'A man who'd do that's got a real bad habit, Sheriff.'

With an equally straight face Ike said, 'Go suck eggs.'

That was the extent of their conversation until Jered, still walking ahead, stopped and raised an arm. It was dark; if the moon had fattened any since last night it was not noticeable. He barely raised his voice when he said, 'Close, Sheriff. It could be a bear but I don't think so. Bears don't have no hooves to stamp with.'

The constable dismounted bringing the carbine with him. Although he strained to hear something, there was not a sound.

Jered handed over his reins and silently faded ahead through darkness. The constable stood hip-shot waiting. It was a fairly long wait. When Jered appeared something, poor light, mammoth trees, something anyway made him look a foot taller than he was, and that was almighty tall.

He got close to speak in almost a whisper. 'We found the rode-down mare, Mister Bowen ... But no rider. A saddle, blanket an' bridle in the grass but no saddlebags ... I don't have no mother, but if I did have I wouldn't want her to cry tonight, so I'll slip back where the horse is croppin' grass while you circle up an' around, come toward the horse from above ... Sheriff, if you make a sound –'

'Jered, I didn't come down in the last rain!'

The tall man turned away. Isaac had to find low

tree limbs to tie their animals to before beginning his encircling hike. He had his Winchester to push aside low limbs.

The night had turned chilly back yonder somewhere. Ike was unaware of this until he was walking uphill on an angling course.

When he finally looked southward where a bay animal was standing stone-still with its head up, little ears pointing in the direction Ike assumed the saloonman was skulking, he noticed even in poor light that the horse was as tucked up in the flank as a gutted snowbird. It was a wonder the animal had come this far. Until the mare shifted slightly to fully face the man she scented but could not see, Ike did not notice the pronounced limp.

He also made out the place where someone had flung aside his riding equipment. The saddle boot was empty but the tightly-rolled bedroll was still behind the cantle.

Nothing happened for almost fifteen minutes. Neither the lawman or the saloonman were in any hurry to approach the mare and expose themselves, but eventually the tall man spoke crooningly to the wary animal and moved beside a large tree where he was about as visible as a phantom. Another long wait ensued during which the constable also came southward and Jered quietly said, 'She's alone.'

Ike still moved with caution. This was one of those situations where a mistake could fix things for a shot-individual to bleed to death even though, had he been down in Cedarton, a shattered vein could be cared for in time. They had a very competent midwife down there who could cure collar galls on harness animals, deliver hung-up babies, stitch bad cuts and tie off bad bleedings.

Her name was Marge O'Leary; she was a long distance from where Constable Bowen finally walked over to the mare, who was startled to find that there had been two phantoms. But even if she'd been able to flee, she was not the kind of critter who feared two-legged creatures very much.

Jered quartered like a hunting dog. He ignored the mare until he had read enough sign to know what he needed to know. Then he came over, looked the mare over and said, 'If I didn't have no other reason for killing this son of a bitch, the way he treated this animal would be enough.'

Jered stepped back looking eastward. 'Still the same direction, Sheriff, east in a straight line ... They got a destination, I'd bet my saloon on that ... Well?'

'This is cougar country an' she can't run.'

'She'll slow us down, Sheriff.'

'We're already slowed down. I'll fetch the horses.'

While Ike was gone the saloonman ran an exploring hand down the mare's favoured leg, lifted the hoof, leaned so close his nose was almost touching, then dropped the foot, dug out a wicked-bladed clasp knife, raised the hoof and went to work.

When the constable returned Jered held up his open palm with a sharp-edged diamond-hard piece of granite on it.

Ike wagged his head. 'Dumb bastard. Didn't even look.'

Jered dropped the small stone. 'Maybe he's a

good murderer, but he sure don't know beans about lame horses.'

The mare still limped. It would be some time before she recovered from the stone bruise caused by a rock between her hoof and the steel shoe.

They left her in open country. Maybe she couldn't out-run a predator, but at least she could scent or see one coming; her chances were about fifty-fifty.

They pushed ahead until a streak of sickly grey light showed in the far-away east. It was now as cold as it would be until the following day at this time.

The trail was easy to follow. Jered only occasionally glanced downward. He was more concerned about being in open country after sunrise.

Ike said, 'If I recollect right, there's a cow outfit where they could get fresh horses about three, four miles east an' a mite south.'

Jered was cheeking a fresh cud and could not speak for a moment. 'How big an outfit?' he asked, clearly speculating on what they might find.

'It's been a couple of years, Jered. It's run by an elderly couple with two grown sons.'

Jered spat, straightened in the saddle and looked very grave. 'Sheriff, wolves like this bunch eat a place like that alive, same as they did the Garfield place, and hell, Neil Garfield had more riders.'

'Not when they struck, Jered.'

The tall man said no more. He pulled his neck down inside the upturned collar of his coat and rode in bleak silence watching for buildings to appear.

They did appear, but not until the sun was teetering on the rim of the world, by which time the tall man had got rid of his cud, and halted dead still leaning on his saddle horn.

The constable spoke softly. 'It don't feel right. There should be smoke from the kitchen stove pipe.'

Jered nodded. 'Sheriff, you ride on in. I'll go see where they went from here.'

'Maybe they're still down there, Jered.'

The tall man shrugged. He did not believe for a minute the raiders were still down there. He did not want to look at what his heart told him he would see if he rode with the constable into that silent, haunted-looking ranch yard.

4

A Meeting

Ike's first sight was of a large brindle dog sprawled in death in front of the barn. His head had been blown apart.

The place was as silent as a tomb except for some chickens behind a tall wire fence which coyotes could not climb.

The constable tied up out front of the barn, freed the tie-down over his six-gun and looked first inside the barn and out back where some pole corrals had been built.

There were two horses out back, not in the corral but standing listlessly beside it. Both were tucked up, sweat-stained and Ike knew if he approached them and placed his thumb and forefinger in the centre of their backs over the kidneys and pushed, both animals would have flinched.

He had no doubt who had abandoned those animals. He also did not doubt they would not have been abandoned unless replacements had been taken.

He went slowly up through the barn where daylight had not yet reached and nearly stumbled over some torn-open grain sacks behind which he saw a hand and arm.

The dead man hadn't been shot, he had been struck over the head from behind by someone with a powerful arm. His skull looked lopsided, his eyes were wide open staring straight up. He was old.

He hadn't been armed; men rarely wore sidearms in their own barns.

Ike went across to the main-house. The second corpse was of an elderly woman. She had been shot as she left the house to cross the porch. It was a blessing that she had never known what had struck her. The bullet was dead centre in her chest. Her hair was pulled up in a bun, she had what looked like flour on her hands and arms. Her apron was typical; it had been made of flour sacking with the maker's name bleached out.

Ike stepped past, hovered in the doorway surveying the devastation resulting from wild ransacking, moved into the parlour, side-stepped an overturned leather sofa, a heavy chair on its side, went to the kitchen and stopped in the doorway. Dishes were in a large pan atop the stove, food on a sideboard was where the woman had left it. A broken chair lay near the kindling box.

Ike went through the rest of the house expecting to find another corpse or two. What he found was ruin and destruction, ransacked drawers, broken furniture, three windows which had been shattered from inside, but no dead people.

He returned to the yard, leaned on a porch

upright, studied the empty land for sign of Jered Salte, and saw instead a distant rider leading a pack animal heading for the yard from the north.

Jered came from around the house leading his horse. He too saw the rider with the pack horse. He asked what Ike had found as he saw the older woman face down and quickly looked away.

Ike told him about the old man in the barn, the worn-out saddle animals out back, and as the rider came closer, he said, 'There's nothin' we can tell him that he can't figure out for himself … I'll get my horse.'

Jered was in front of the main-house holding his horse when the rider stopped, sat a long time looking at the brindle dog, then raised his eyes to Jered and without haste drew and cocked his six-gun.

From the man's right side in the barn doorway Ike said, 'There was five of 'em. I'm the constable from Cedarton. We been on their trail for a couple of days. That there is Jered Salte who owns the saloon in Cedarton … There's a dead man behind me in the barn.'

The rider turned his head. He was younger than the constable, rough-complexioned with a lipless slash of a mouth and calm, unwavering eyes. 'Old gent, is he, Constable?'

'Yes.'

'… Anyone else get hurt?'

'There's an older woman on the porch, shot through the heart.'

The rider dismounted, left his animals and crossed the yard with long strides. Jered moved aside. The younger man went part way up the steps and halted. 'Maw,' he said quietly, then sank to the steps as though his legs had turned to putty.

Jered led his animal to the barn where Constable Bowen was ready to leave. They rode out of the yard on a southwesterly course, with nothing to say for several miles, then Jered said, 'Two fresh horses ain't enough. They need three more.'

Ike said nothing. The direction the raiders had taken was more westward than southward. They would ride many miles before they came to another ranch. Ike began to wonder if they really knew Cedar Valley or whether they were not riding out of the valley. One thing he was sure of, there were two cow outfits on their route. Each one had hired riders, were owned by men who were unlikely to be caught after dark the way those old folks had been caught back yonder.

Jered was squinting against sunlight when he said, 'Up to now I thought we could guess where they're goin' an' leave off trackin', which is always a slow business, an' maybe hurry up enough to get a sighting … But now I got no idea where they're going.'

Ike was not as concerned about the outlaws as he was about their horses. When they made a mid-day halt beside a creek and chewed jerky, he mentioned getting fresh animals.

Jered nodded and gestured. 'Where?'

'North a few miles at the Glascock outfit. I know Mister Glascock pretty well.'

Jered slumped in willow shade. 'North? Sheriff, they're not goin' north.'

'I know that. We got to sacrifice time for fresh horses or we're goin' to wind up on foot.'

'They're good for a while yet.'

Ike threw up his hands.

They left the creek following tracks a blind man could have followed. Under better circumstances they could have picked up the gait for a few miles, but they didn't. A horse lacked a lot of being a machine, even though the marauders did not appear to know it. They had not spared their animals since Ike and Jered had picked up the trail and they still were not.

Mid-day came and went, the land remained empty except for an occasional small band of grazing cattle. By evening they were riding very tired horses. Ike said nothing and neither did the tall man. When they were halted by night gloom and settled down to camp the saloonman's mood was bleak.

'The trouble with trackin' sons of bitches like this bunch is that a man's always behind 'em … Sheriff, if you know this country …'

'I don't know it real well.'

'We got to figure where they're goin' an' somehow get around in front of 'em, or we're goin' to be shaggin' them forever.'

'You said it wasn't goin' to be no picnic, Jered; you said it could be done.'

The tall man showed irritability not anger when he said, 'It *can* be done, Sheriff, but what bothers me is how many more folk clubbed or shot at night without even a suspicion do we have to step over?'

Ike's reply was based on what had been

bothering him all day. 'Fresh horses, Jered. Somewhere down here we got to get fresh horses.'

'Where?'

'Damned if I know, but if we see a yard we got to take time to swap horses.'

What happened was that while they did not see a yard or buildings, they came out of a low draw with the sun in their faces not a hundred yards from a small band of someone's barefoot loose-stock still stiff from a cold night. They caught two horses, both bays with white hair at the withers from old galls. Neither was young but both were muscled-up, strong animals in their prime.

They had shoulder brands on the left side which looked like a turkey track, something they ignored as they hastily rigged out the bays, left their own animals to mingle with the loose-stock and filthy, unshaved, weary though they were, strong horse-flesh under them gave each man a fresh outlook.

They warmed out their fresh animals then picked up the gait and held them to it for several miles. They were still far behind but at least with luck they could get a little closer.

The turkey track animals were good using horses. When someone discovered they were gone, he was goin' to swear a blue streak.

They did not stop to rest. They chewed jerky in the saddle, made no attempt to rest the animals until near the day's end because aside from trying to close the distance they did not come across a creek until late afternoon.

After off-saddling, allowing their 'borrowed' mounts to drink and graze, the constable looked at his companion and laughed. 'Jered, you look like hell.'

The bean-pole tall man looked down his nose. 'I never expected to win no beauty prize. If the feller who owns these horses happens to ride out to see his loose-stock, we might have some trouble down our back trail.' The tall man continued to regard his companion. 'I got a feelin' that badge ain't goin' to keep you from gettin' hung. This far from anywhere the law's got a habit of bein' very simple in its homespun justice.'

They only rested until midnight. Jered was convinced the renegades would not change course; they were making an angling approach to the mountains far to the east which girdled Cedar Valley.

It was a guess but a shrewd one. The more Constable Bowen rode with the saloonman, the more convinced he became that Salte wasn't just following tracks, he was reacting in the way outlaws acted.

They halted atop a dusky ridge just before sunrise, something they would not have done if it had been daylight. Ike was chewing a cigar when he raised his arm. 'Camp fire. You see it?'

Jered grunted, urged his turkey track horse down the slope and rode without haste directly toward the distant flicker of light. 'Some damned cowhand,' he grumbled. 'Most likely out huntin' someone's strays. Where's the nearest ranch?'

Ike had to shake his head. 'I'd guess north. I've only been this far up the valley a couple of times an' that was years ago.'

They were less than a mile from the light which was beginning to look feeble as dawn crept closer. Both riders strained to get a sighting. They were in country which had erosion arroyos, some fairly deep, all with grassy sides indication those arroyos had been made many years earlier.

Each time they went down into an arroyo they lost sight of the light. In one arroyo Jered growled. 'Put that damned badge in your pocket.'

They topped out with Ike removing his badge. They were now close enough to make out a dozing horse in hobbles. The horse would pick up their scent before long.

Two tie-downs were jerked free as they got close enough to see a lumpy bedroll beside the fire. Ike shook his head. He'd done what the stranger had done many times; get the fire lighted and climb back where it was warm for a while.

The horse jerked erect facing them. They waited for him to nicker but he did not make a sound, he simply stood with his head up, his ears pointing, for all the world like a statue.

The man in the bedroll heard them. He rolled over and sat up rubbing his eyes. His hair was every which way, his six-gun and belt were coiled within easy reach. His boots were close to the dying small fire.

Ike called ahead. 'If you got some coffee we won't tell the boss about you sleepin' the day away.'

The man twisted out of his blanket-roll reaching for his boots. Jered made a clucking sound; if their positions had been reversed he'd have reached for his gunbelt first.

The stranger stamped into his boots, pitched several twigs on the fire and faced around as Jered and the constable halted to sit, hands atop their horns, gazing at him.

The stranger was weathered and lined but he was no older than either of his visitors. He said, 'Coffee an' sourdough bread harder'n a rock … Turkey track? I seen some horses with that mark some time back.'

Jered rolled his eyes. The damned fool still hadn't picked up his shellbelt and weapon. Ike dismounted first, as he stepped to the head of his horse Jered also came down.

The hobbled horse showed a shrunken gut. He was still strong but only in appearance. He had been used hard for a long time.

Ike asked if the stranger worked for some nearby outfit and got an answer he didn't expect. 'No; I'm just travellin' through.'

Jered was not looking at the tousle-headed man, he was looking at the ground where at least five riders had arrived at this spot some time before. Beyond the camp he could see where the other riders had gone on, in the direction of the distant mountains. He asked if the stranger had seen anyone out here, and got a negative head-shake.

Jered stood gazing at the stranger. 'Mister, what's your name?'

'Bart Smith. What's yours?'

'Jered Salte – with an e. My friend here is Constable Ike Bowen from Cedarton. We been shaggin' some raiders. Tracked 'em right to this spot, Mister Smith.'

For five seconds there was not a sound before Bart Smith made a gesture with both hands flung wide, 'I ain't seen no riders. Maybe if they come this way they went past in the night.'

Jered slowly wagged his head. 'Their sign led us right here, Mister Smith. Right where you're camped.' Jered jutted his jaw. 'Over yonder is where they rode on … Mind my horse, Constable. I want to see how many horses rode away from here … I'm willin' to bet good money it was four.'

Ike took the reins without taking his eyes off the tousle-headed, weathered man, who watched Jered cross the camp, and flicked a glance at his coiled shellbelt with the leathered six-gun on top.

Ike's unblinking gaze never wavered. The stranger twisted away from Ike and started to put his hand in a trouser pocket. Ike warned him. 'Keep 'em both where I can see 'em, Mister Smith.'

Jered faced around from the opposite side of the camp. 'Four, Constable, like I figured.' Jered strolled back watching Bart Smith with his head lowered. 'How long ago did your friends leave?'

'I told you. I'm just passin' through. I never seen no other riders.'

Jered halted close and looked down into the other man's face. 'Sheriff, we finally got one.'

Ike told the stranger to empty his pockets. Bart Smith obeyed but with clear reluctance. He had gold coins tied in a small handkerchief, the kind women used, not men. He also had several gold rings and a small ivory-handled .41 calibre belly gun. It had initials engraved on the backstrap. S.H.

Ike was holding the little gun when his memory

offered something he had forgotten. He looked at Bart Smith. 'Those old folks that was killed at a ranch back yonder – do you know what their name was?'

'What people? How many times I got to tell you; I'm just passin' through.'

'The old gent that had his head crushed from behind … His name was John Hamilton. The old woman shot dead on her front porch was his wife, Sara Hamilton.' Ike held the small weapon where the stranger could see the initials. He lost colour but started to repeat what he had said before about just passing through when Jered moved without haste to back-hand the stranger knocking him on his back within a foot of the little blazing fire. The man scrambled to his feet, eyes wild, body tense.

Ike reversed the little belly-gun, cocked it and aimed it. 'Where did your friends go? … One more lie an' I'll blow your head open. *Where are they heading!*'

Bart Smith seemed mesmerised by the snout of the small gun ten feet from his chest.

Jered growled at Ike. 'Through the belly. It won't kill him right off; he'll still be able to talk.'

Ike tipped the gun a notch. Bart Smith spoke so rapidly his words ran together. 'There's an old man's got a stump ranch against them mountains east from here. Porter Caulfield's related to him. That's where they figure to rest up for a spell.'

'Do you know where this place is; do you know the old man?'

'No. Porter told us about it when we come up from the south to raid through the country. None of us ever been here before.'

'You're Bart Smith.'

'My real name is –'

'It's not goin' to matter,' Jered exclaimed. 'Who are the others?'

'... I'll make a trade with you. I'll tell you what I know an' all you got to do is look the other way while I saddle up.'

For the first time since Constable Bowen had known the saloonman, Jered smiled. 'All right, Mister Smith; name them for us.'

'Porter Caulfield, he knew where to raid in this country, Terry Bligh, John Bryan, Pat Ruggles ... An' me.'

Ike eased the hammer down and pocketed the little lady's gun, probably a gift from her dead husband in the barn back yonder.

5

The Bear Trap

Jered got the fire burning, used the renegade's coffee and hardtack bread to make a meal. The outlaw also had two tins of milk and some sardines in his saddle pockets.

It was a bizarre first meal of the new day but anything beat a snow bank.

The constable asked how the outlaw happened to be alone and got a simple answer. Evidently the outlaw had decided to be cooperative though he had to know how close he was to the edge of eternity.

'I just couldn't make it no further. I dislocated a hip some months back. It seemed to be on the mend, but this last trip, on the move day'n night ... Couldn't get on m'horse no more.' The renegade addressed Ike. 'About that belly gun – I found it in a box at that ranch back yonder, but I didn't shoot nobody. Porter snuck into the barn an' hid until the old man come down to do his chores. He hit him over the head with a single tree ... The old lady come out … Terry was bringin' in two horses from out back when the old lady come out onto the porch. I figure she was goin' to call to the old man about breakfast bein' ready … Terry shot her head-on.'

Jered put a cold look on the outlaw. 'An' all you done was set around watchin'.'

'No. I helped Pat switch horses.'

'Who was ridin' the lame mare?'

'Terry Bligh. She come up lame after we …' the outlaw faltered.

'Go on; after you raided the ranch where you killed two women.'

The outlaw stared into the fire. 'I held the horses.'

Jered was holding a cup of hot coffee. He considered it briefly then flung it into the renegade's face as he stood up snarling. 'Ike, I lost my appetite. Let's finish here an' get to riding.'

The outlaw was mopping off hot coffee with a filthy bandana. That coffee had been too hot to drink. He was in pain until he cleared his eyes and saw them standing over him. The pain seemed to stop at once.

'I told you everything,' he whined. 'I been real helpful.'

Jered nodded about that. 'Yes sir, Mister Smith. I never met a feller who was so helpful gettin' himself killed. *Stand up!*'

The renegade's attitude changed. He did not arise, he snarled and hurled himself at the nearest pair of legs, which belonged to Jered Salte. The tall man went down hard. The outlaw sprang past Ike diving for his holstered Colt.

Ike stepped ahead, caught the outlaw by the back

of his shirt and using all his strength, lifted the man and flung him away from the shellbelt.

Jered got back upright, looked at the other men, calmly dusted himself off and turned with a six-gun in his fist. Ike started to speak as Jered fired, not once but four times. Each bullet punched the renegade along the ground. After the first shot the man was limp as a rag.

Jered re-loaded while echoes were still chasing one another, slammed the weapon into its holster, kicked dirt over the fire and turned his back on the constable as he went to his horse, swung up and sat coldly considering the man he had killed.

The sun was climbing. The air was as clear as glass. Their horses had had a respite and were prepared for whatever came next, which was part of the resigned acceptance of horses; they were unable to predict what the two-legged things on their backs were liable to do.

Not until the sun was high with the easterly mountains seeming to retreat as they crossed toward them, did either man speak, then Jered said, 'He had that comin' an' a lot more.'

Ike rode in silence.

Jered eventually looked around. 'Well?' he said, almost making a challenge of it.

Ike gazed at the saloonman. 'What you got a chip on your shoulder about?'

Jered spoke bluntly. 'It was murder an' you're a lawman.'

'Not murder, Jered, justice ... I wish there was more trees in this part of the valley. Another few miles an' if they're in the uplands loafin' they'll be able to see us coming.'

Jered tucked some tobacco into a cheek and squinted ahead. 'It's still a hell of a distance, Sheriff.'

'See that bosk of black oaks? We'd better hole up in there until nightfall,' Ike stated.

They covered another mile or so before entering the stand of oak trees, of which several were larger around than a man's body which meant they were probably not too far from being a couple of hundred years old. The other trees were not quite as impressive, but they cast shade and helped provide a good place to lie over for a spell.

There was no water but there was grass, which seemed to satisfy the turkey track horses. Ike tipped his hat, got comfortable and slept. Jered shed his cud, leaned in oak shade and for a long time gazed back in the direction from which they had come.

He regretted nothing. He had been riding several days with a fire of hatred in his belly. Later generations would never approve, but by that time he, the simple things men like Jered Salte – with an e – believed in, as well as men like Jered Salte, would be dead, which was probably a good thing. They lacked the temperament for defending their convictions; if arguments got hot enough they settled them the same way Jered had settled the hash of Bart Smith – if that was his name, which was something else that did not matter.

An old raccoon waddled in out of the heat, saw a pair of smelly two-legged critters and halted to raise up, sniff and stare from coal-black eyes. Jered spoke to the animal. 'Sorry, partner, but we got nothin' with salt in it.'

The furry, fat animal continued to regard Jered. Raccoons would fight a buzz saw. They feared men less than they feared dogs, moreover they were curious animals. Only one range critter was more curious – antelope.

Jered fished forth his plug of molasses-cured, tore off a splinter and tossed it. The 'coon's shiny wet nose wiggled. It had no idea what the man had tossed toward it but because it knew what honey was, it associated the sweet smell with something edible, waddled over and ate the chewing tobacco. Jered watched and waited. The first chew he'd ever had made him so sick he had heaved his boot straps. The 'coon raised up on its hind legs waiting for the next toss.

Jered obliged, the bit of tobacco fell short. Without hesitation the 'coon waddled over, picked up the treat in both paws and ate it while studying Jered.

A dry voice came from beneath Ike's hatbrim. 'You got a friend.'

'I'm waitin' for him to throw up.'

'Be a long wait, Jered. Them little devils can eat a whole plug.'

Ike pushed his hat back. Movement from a different direction made the 'coon look around, drop down and scuttle away.

Their horses were full as ticks standing head to tail in warm shade, the custom of horses in fly country; a swishing tail at both ends discouraged bot flies from entering their nostrils to lay eggs in horses' bellies. In this case it was more instinct than necessity because flies did not stay in dark, shady places.

Jered rose and walked to the western side of their shady place. After a while he returned to say, 'If these horses had belonged to me I'd be coming along our back trail like a hound dog. Or that feller back where the old folks got killed. I'd be lookin' for us too.'

Ike sat up, scratched, re-set his hat and squinted past tree tops seeking the position of the sun, which he did not find, so he judged how much time was left in the day by shadows.

'Couple more hours, Jered.'

'That's goin' to put us close to the easterly foothills by morning – I hope. Because I got no desire to have them bastards see us comin'.'

A faint mist was coming into the afternoon which neither man noticed. Later, with dusk diminishing visibility they saddled up and left the oaks. From here on, except for patches of pines close to the foothills, there was no protection from watching eyes, but they had decided to take the risk, which actually was not very great; when the mountains were only barely visible to them, two horsemen would be just as invisible to watchers.

The tracks were there; four riders on animals that scuffed dust with their hind feet from weariness, but Jered only read the sign until dusk faded to night, after which he did not dismount to read it as he'd done before.

Where, exactly, the stump ranch was they could deduce from what sign they had seen; it did not deviate from a direct approach to a notch in the lower foothills. Of course the tracks could change course later but Jered did not believe they would.

However, the area they were aiming toward was about a mile wide. The renegades could change course up there several degrees to the north or south.

They did not worry about that; the direction they were travelling could change, but probably not until the foothills or the timbered country above it made a change necessary, by which time Jered could lead his horse to follow the sign, which would be slow going but providing they had cover, and also providing the renegades had not left the country, there should be contact by sunrise.

Ike wanted a smoke. He had three stogies left. He also wanted a drink of water, which was something he could not control, but he could forget about the cigar.

Jered was quiet most of the way, but his head was up and moving; he was alert and wary, an attitude which became more noticeable as they finally were able to make out the awesome height and thickness of the mountains.

He was watching ahead when he said, 'If it's a stump ranch like that dead son of a bitch said, it won't be very far into the mountains.'

Ike nodded without speaking. He was wrinkling his nose. It seemed there was a very faint aroma of tobacco smoke in the night. They were still a fair distance from the foothills. He sniffed, looked around without being able to see much farther ahead than a hundred yards or so, and finally leaned to brush Jered's arm, put a finger to his lips and make an exaggerated sniffing motion. Jered stopped, raised his head and looked blankly at the constable. He had smelled nothing.

Ike was about to squeeze his horse when the aroma came again, more noticeable this time. Jered picked it up, the windless night had enough movement for the scent to reach him. He tried to figure out the direction it was coming from.

Ike abruptly swung to the ground with his Winchester. Jered did the same. Ike pointed northeasterly. They led their horses as soundless as ghosts. Although the ground had been becoming gravelly the closer they got to the mountains, while steel shod horses made noise over stony soil, barefoot horses did not.

The scent became stronger, strong enough for Ike to suspect its pungency came from a mixture of tobacco and kinikinnick, the mixture of men who used native herbs to make their tobacco last until they reached a settlement.

They halted when the aroma was strongest. Ike handed his reins to Jered and walked carefully ahead. There was no light because the smoker was down in an arroyo that ran perpendicular to the foothills. His fire was no more than several twigs. It would have been just about impossible to see even if it hadn't been in the gulch.

Ike heard him, crept to the edge of the gully, got flat down and carefully poked his head over the crumbly bank.

Whoever he was, he had a bear trap nearly as large as the man crouching over it was as he ratcheted the jaws open. Nearby barely distinguishable by weak moonlight, was a dead young goat.

Ike watched the hunched figure who was smoking a small pipe which he puffed between ratchets to spring the trap wide. It was one of those large, steel, enormously strong traps with a big chain leading from it to a nearby boulder only a very powerful bear could budge.

Ike waited until the man in the gully had set his trap before easing off the lock on the ratchet and was ready to put the dead goat in place before he stood up in plain sight.

But the trapper was engrossed in what he was doing. At this particular point in his undertaking, unless the goat was placed on the pan with extreme care, the trap would spring.

Ike's judgement was that the trapper either liked to live dangerously or was a damned fool. No one he had ever seen baiting bear traps ever released the lock until after the bait had been put in place.

He scarcely breathed as he watched the man slide the carcass to the pan from beneath the serrated jaws. He was very careful, moved with infinite caution, got the little carcass gently placed on the pan, and drew back on his haunches to examine his handiwork.

Ike said, 'One of these times it'll take your arm off.'

The man looked up. 'Pat? When you set as many of these things as I have, sonny, I'll be glad to listen to you … What you doin' down here, anyway? I thought after shoein' them horses you'd be wore out.'

Ike slid down the crumbly bank, saw the squatting man begin to stand up, aimed his Colt and said, 'Not a sound. Not a damned sound.' He cocked the weapon for emphasis.

The trapper was old, gaunt, lined and weathered. He had very pale eyes. His pipe went out as he faced the younger man. 'Who are you?' he asked in a reedy voice. The old man had a long-barrelled six-gun in a holster with the bottom left open for the lengthy barrel to extrude. He couldn't have made a fast draw if he'd wanted to, the barrel was too long.

'Are your friends at the cabin?' Ike asked.

The old man stood still and silent staring at the man he had mistaken for someone else.

Ike gestured with his Colt. 'Go down the draw until you can climb out. I'll be right behind you.'

Finally, the old man found his tongue. He did not appear the least bit afraid when he said, 'You pull that trigger, sonny, an' they'll come down on you like a rash.'

Ike went close, put up his weapon, punched the old man in the back over the kidneys to get him moving, and each time he hesitated he punched him again.

Where they left the arroyo there was a good game trail, narrow but gently angling from the arroyo to flat ground above. When they halted up above the old man had something else to say.

'If you're lookin' for shelter, I got a houseful.'

Ike punched the old man in the direction where Jered was holding the horses. When he saw Jered he looked him up and down before saying, 'Mister, in the dark you'd pass for Abe Lincoln. How tall are you?'

Jered gazed dispassionately at the older man. 'Ike, he's too old for ... Is this the feller who has the stump ranch?'

'That's my guess.' Ike tried once more for a name. 'Who are you?'

'Just an old buffler hunter who lives by himself an' likes it that way. Who's this tall feller?'

Jered was no more impressed with the old man's toughness than he'd been with anyone like the old man. He leaned down, took a handful of shirting with his left hand and slapped the old man first one side of the head then on the other side.

When he stepped back and released the old man, he held out a long finger like a gun barrel. 'One more time, pappy, then I'll snap your neck like a twig. What's your name?'

The old man hadn't been hurt by the slapping but he had lost some of his bravado, probably more because of the intimidating height of the tall unsmiling man staring down at him, than because of Ike's pistol behind him. 'Jake Caulfield,' he said.

Jered looked over the old man's head at Ike, who put up his six-gun. Jered looked down again. 'Is Porter your son?'

'Son? Porter's my nephew out of my sister's oldest boy. You know Porter, do you?'

'I come a long way to make his acquaintance, Mister Caulfield.'

'He ain't goin' to like you two jumpin' me in the dark an' beatin' on me.'

Jered found his plug, gnawed off a corner

without taking his eyes off the older man. When he was ready he looked across the old man's head as he said, 'We got somethin' to trade with, Sheriff.'

Jake Caulfield gave a start and whirled to glare at the constable. Before he could erupt Ike tapped his chest with a stiff finger. 'First, we're goin' to talk, Mister Caulfield, then Jered'll cut your throat because we can't leave you behind when we go up to the house ... Unless you do what's best for your health.'

Jered lifted Caulfield's ancient shooting iron, examined it, shook his head and flung it away. He then brought forth the big-bladed knife he used to carve tobacco with and opened it. 'Set down,' he told old Caulfield, who obeyed instantly. 'Now then, grandpa, you got four visitors have you?'

Caulfield bobbed his head without making a sound.

Jered leaned down with the knife blade forward. 'I used to keep it sharp so's when I slashed it went deep real fast. Lately I ain't had time to sharpen it, so I expect it won't slice as much as it'll tear ... Mister Caulfield, we want your nephew and his friends, and unless you want to find out how dull this knife is, you'll help us ... It's up to you.'

The old man's courage decreased the longer he listened to the tall man leaning down, as expressionless as a rock, but whisker-stubbled, unwashed, very earnest looking.

'... We're waitin', Mister Caulfield. It's dull but it'll cut.'

The old man swung his head toward Ike who was standing like a statue looking steadily back. There did not appear to be a shred of mercy in either of the faces of the soiled, rumpled-looking strangers. Old Caulfield was crowding eighty, which was plenty long for a man to live, but he wasn't convinced of that.

6

A Frightening Interruption

The old man had lived a long time. He was not without fear, something which induced common-sense caution, so his many years had also taught him when to fire and when to fall back. This was one of those fall-back times. His companions looked filthy, lean and merciless.

His initial mistake was to believe they were acquaintances of his nephew. They had acted like they were. Evidence of his mistake was within ten inches of his throat and while the tall man had said it was dull, it did not look dull to the old man.

But it was a hard decision for the tough old man, so when he finally spoke his voice was harsh. 'They're at my house. I sold 'em new shoes for their animals. They figure to leave come sunup.'

Jered relaxed a little. 'How do we get 'em?'

This time the old man's lipless slit of a mouth became taut. 'That's up to you,' he rasped.

Jered leaned, made a slight scratch with his knife and softly said. 'One last time, Mister Caulfield.

How do we get 'em?'

The opportunity for deception was great and the old man hadn't become sly over the years, he had been born that way. 'You could go up there across the opening. They know I come down here to trap that danged bear that's been a nuisance for the past few months. Just walk across the open place.'

Ike slowly shook his head. Jered did too. The old man's tongue darted out and back before he spoke again. 'They're inside eatin' an' fixin' to leave. You could slip around the house an' come in from behind. There ain't no window in the back wall.'

The old man had barely stopped speaking when a tremendous roar blew the stillness apart, it was accompanied by the sound of a steel chain being stretched to its limit. The second roar lacked the sound of surprise and pain, it was the full-throated bellow of an enraged large bear.

Ike straightened up as he pocketed the knife and faced in the direction of the arroyo. The old man's goat-baited trap had worked, and from the sounds of threshing and bellowing the carnivore he had caught was large and very angry.

The horses would have spun and fled if Ike hadn't jerked them hard. Even then they pulled back, swung sideways and back, rolled their eyes in mortal terror and fought to get free.

The situation changed abruptly. While Ike fought to prevent the horses from breaking away, Jered stood near the old man trying to guess from the mad bellowing whether the trap would hold or not.

It wouldn't; the old man's choice of a huge

boulder to hold his trap by its chain was sound, except that the enraged animal caught in the trap, whether the chain and boulder would have held or not, was a very large and wildly enraged bear.

Jered heard the boulder shift. A moment later he heard loose chain snapping like a whip.

There was no more formidable creature alive than a large bear which would top seven feet when he stood at his full height, and which could weigh as much as a ton. Angry, his fury and strength doubled. If either of the men from Cedarton had time to consider it, they might have been awed by the rage that injured bear was evincing as he struck large boulders, sent them tumbling, and snapped trees as he tumbled and rolled trying to get the massive trap loose.

Jered got their carbines. Ike took his with one hand still fighting to prevent the horses from fleeing with the other hand. He had no illusions; if the mammoth old bear came up out of the arroyo he would smell horses and men. In his present mood he would tear into pieces any warm-blooded creature he could scent.

There were many stories of men emptying guns into enraged bears and still being mauled to death before the bears succumbed.

Men's shouts were audible between the injured animal's thunderous roars. Ike released the horses. he and Jered would be afoot, but the situation had changed; they no longer needed the horses, in fact the ensuing action would make horses a burden. Those shouting men were coming through the night on the run.

Ike gauged the shouts until he was satisfied the renegades were rushing toward the arroyo where the bear was rolling and writhing, and bellowing. Ike grabbed the old man, half spun him around and called to Jered. 'The house!'

The old man writhed and squawked in the constable's grip. Ike cuffed him under the ribs with his carbine. The old man doubled over with pain.

Ike yanked him upright and spoke into his face. 'Lead the way to the house.'

They had barely begun moving when a man's scream followed by three rapid pistol shots warned them that the bear was no longer in the arroyo.

After the last gunshot there was silence for about half a minute, then the bear roared again. Every creature, including two-legged ones, who heard that noise had hair standing straight up. Poor visibility made the situation worse.

Ike and Jered knew, as presumably did the renegades, that whether the screaming man had hit the bear with his wild shooting, none of the injuries had been fatal because the bear bellowed again. He was moving, the chain told his enemies that, but it was difficult to figure in which direction. His bellowing continued, it sounded very close, too close in fact, so Ike, with the old man in his grip, started moving westerly in a large circle.

If the bear's rage hadn't been so wild he would have stopped bellowing. If he had done that he would have heard moving men in the night.

He did just as well despite darkness; bears did not have good vision but their senses of smell and hearing were very good.

While Ike and Jered hiked briskly on a rounding westerly course, with old Caulfield no longer requiring restraint, it seemed the bear was moving parallel to them, possibly on the scent of one of the outlaws, or perhaps all of them.

The enraged animal had the initiative. Ike heard men running. They seemed to be ahead of the bear, who normally could have overtaken the fleetest of them. Bears looked awkward but they could out-run the fastest man and given the chance, some horses.

Old Caulfield stood crouched and listening. He said, 'If they don't shoot that old bear, he'll beat them to the cabin.'

Ike punched the old man. The three of them continued on their rounding discernible against a background of big trees and, farther back, the kind of a mountain formation that blocked out sightings day or night.

What changed things was that at least one of the renegades had not run toward the house. He was easterly somewhere. When he fired Ike had a feeling this particular outlaw reacted to danger the way most men of his kind did, he got well east of the path the bear was taking with his rattling chain – straight toward the strongest man-scent. He must have been able to see the bear because he only fired once.

The rattling continued for several moments but it seemed to be moving with less haste now, and somewhat erratically, then it stopped altogether.

Jered said, 'Bull's eye,' and began moving again.

They were somewhat south of the house on their

angling northwesterly course. They were able to use the moments of silence around front to get behind the house and approach it walking easterly.

The old man hadn't lied, there were no openings of any kind in the back wall.

The house was old, its log walls with sugar-pine shingles on the roof were a uniform corpse-colour even in darkness.

Someone had laboriously cleared considerable ground completely around the house, which anyone with a lick of sense did when they lived in timber country, particularly fir and pine country. Even a grass fire would make those varieties of timber burn hot and fast, like Roman candles, not so much in winter but certainly in summer.

There were several dilapidated outbuildings and a set of good peeled-log corrals. That bear had made the corralled livestock hit the stringers trying to break out. Now, while the horses were still terrified they continued to move, to test the logs, but without the noise from the bear they were losing some of their fear.

It was the noise the horses made that blanked out the noise of the men behind the house. When they were within a few feet of the rear log wall Ike gripped the old man's shoulder hard and leaned to whisper, 'One damned fool move, Mister Caulfield, an' Jered'll cut your throat.'

The tall man had to lean far down to rest on his Winchester. He had a hunch the man who had killed the bear would try to cross the clearing to the house, so he moved to the south corner and eased around. There was no movement as far as Jered could see. As he stepped back where he could see Ike and the old man, he shook his head. He did not say it but he was about half convinced the shooter had already returned to the house.

He was wrong.

There was conversation inside the house where a smoking lamp was atop a table. The discussion in there was muted by log walls. Ike leaned close to hear, but could not distinguish words.

Somewhere in the lower reaches of the mountains a wolf sounded to the puny moon. It was an eerie sound – always was. Distance didn't make it any more reassuring, but when another wolf answered from closer to the foothills north of the house old Caulfield muttered something about wolves, like bears, could smell a carcass one hell of a distance.

Ike gave the old man a hard punch. 'Not a word you old whelp!'

Jered slipped back down the south side of the house with less caution this time, which he regretted the moment he saw the striding form.

The outlaw was not being careful. He had no reason, yet, to realise there were a pair of manhunters in the area.

Jered was motionless. The outlaw would see him the second he moved. He ran several desperate thoughts through his head and discarded them all. He could shoot the renegade, but one gunshot would warn the men inside, so he had to stand helplessly and watch the bear-shooter reach the door, disappear inside and slam the door after himself.

Ike listened to Jered's whispering without commenting. All four outlaws were now safe behind log walls ... Maybe not; that man who had fired wild and who had screamed might never have made it. But it really did not matter a whole lot whether there were three or four of them.

Ike stepped behind the old man to whisper to Jered. 'Set the horses loose,' he said.

They forced the old man to go with them to the corrals where excited animals softly snorted at their scent, not really all that afraid of men, but still nervous. Bears ate carrion; their smell carried a considerable distance and lingered.

They reached the corrals when lamplight shone past the opened front door. The man who stepped swiftly away from being backgrounded halted against the front log wall, pressing flat and motionless. They could make him out, he was average height and thickly set-up. That was all they could make out.

After a while he walked over where almost a ton of stinking, maimed bear lay dead. They heard him jostle the trap but could not see what he was doing until he straightened back and stood looking down for a moment before turning back to the house.

Jered leaned down. 'Which one was that?' he whispered to the old man, and got a prompt reply, 'Terry Bligh.' The old man paused a moment then also said, 'It was him shot the old woman on her porch.'

'You wasn't there; how do you know that?'

'I didn't have to be there. They talked about their raids. That's about all they talked about. They got three hunnert in gold money from that raid.'

They were entering the corrals where horses backed away, ducked their heads but didn't snort because the men moved carefully and slowly. Saddles, bridles and blankets had been slung atop peeled log stringers. There were six horses. The old man said, 'Them two sorrels belongs to me,' as though he expected that to make a difference.

Jered stood eyeing the animals. If the old man's animals hadn't been identifiable by colour Jered and Ike could have guessed who they belonged to; they were the only animals in the corral who hadn't been ridden half to death.

The door opened again. This time the renegade was outlined by lamplight for a longer time before he strolled in the direction of the corner of the house. He stopped when a horse nickered.

He stood a moment against the wall peeing, then strolled to the southernmost part of the corral. Ike pushed the old man to the ground, held a finger to his lips in Jered's direction, faded back out of the corral on the north side and with horses and corral poles to shield him, began his stalk.

The outlaw leaned on the topmost stringer eyeing the horses before he stepped back to roll and light a smoke.

He was about to turn away, saw ghostly movement, froze in place searching the area where he was beginning to doubt he had seen anything, and would have moved if a sibilant whisper hadn't warned him not to.

The outlaw dropped his right hand, the fingers were within inches of the arched handle of his six-gun. Ike cocked his Colt. The man's right arm seemed to have become stone.

Jered worked his way past the horses to approach the outlaw from behind. The man heard him but did not move. Jered got close to the inside of the corral and also whispered. 'Lift it out slow an' drop it.'

The outlaw hesitated. Jered leaned across the stringer and cocked his six-gun five feet from the man's head.

He dropped his sidearm.

Ike stepped into full view. He and the outlaw exchanged a long look in silence before Ike stepped aside as he gestured for the man to precede him around to the north side of the corral. When the outlaw got back there old Caulfield spoke with scorn. 'Y'danged idiot, you walked right into it.'

The captive considered the old man from an expressionless face before speaking. 'You double-crossin' old bastard, I'll settle with you.'

Caulfield was stung and would have raised his voice if Jered hadn't returned from the south side of the corral in time to silently warn him not to speak.

The outlaw looked at Jered, he looked up and up, then said, 'Who are you?'

Jered passed over that. 'It's not goin' to matter. What's your name?'

The disgusted old man named the captive. 'John Bryan.'

The renegade glared but Jered held up a stiff finger and wagged it.

Ike herded the two captives northward where a belt of trees intermingled with old stumps, let fading moonlight show downward.

It was getting colder than a witch's tit, sunrise was close. They sat the captive on a stump and asked the old man what this one had bragged about. Because the renegade had threatened old Caulfield he replied with malicious spite.

'Ransackin' a house where there was a girl an' a woman. Him'n my nephew killed 'em both when the old lady refused to say where their money was weaseled away.' Old Caulfield's lipless mouth split into a bleak smile. 'There was another girl; she fought 'em off an' they run for it.'

Ike and Jered gazed at their latest captive. Ike had no difficulty remembering the faces of Neil Garfield's wife and dead daughter.

The chill was very noticeable. Both Jered Salte and the constable had left their coats lashed behind the cantles of their saddles. Jered found a stump to sit on. He appeared to be in no hurry. With daylight close they had achieved their goal of getting up here in darkness.

The rest of their self-imposed chore didn't need darkness, it needed lots of patience, a little luck, and something else which he thought about while considering saddles on the corral stringer.

Ike also sat on a stump. Only the old man stood and moved a little, acting impatient, or maybe hungry and cold to boot, but whatever he felt he kept to himself.

He had two very deadly men sitting close by. He had come to the conclusion that unless he was very careful they would kill him exactly as they clearly intended to do to every renegade in the clearing.

That he was only related to one of the outlaws, and had not, himself, participated in any of the grisly killings his guests had engaged in, might not amount to much; he had given shelter and comfort to killers. There was an iron-clad law about that.

7

A Low Limb, a Strong Rope

John Bryan was different from the man Jered had
repeatedly shot last night a long way west of the
foothill stump ranch. He calmly rolled and lighted
a smoke, ignored old Caulfield with cold dislike,
studied his captors and asked them who they were.

Ike told him; told Bryan he had seen the two
dead Garfield women and the ransacked house.
Bryan trickled smoke as though he was listening to
something of small interest. Eventually he said,
'An' you snuck up'n caught the old bastard.' Bryan
examined the tip of his cigarette. 'You gents will
end up in the same pit as that bear.'

Jered leaned to tap the renegade on the
shoulder. 'Maybe. You won't be around to see that
happen. The man who belonged to that woman,
who was his wife, and his daughter've got riders
hunting for you. Mister, we're goin' to help you
escape 'em. That cowman'll slit your ear an' pull
your arm through – for openers.'

Bryan craned around at the tall man. 'Talk,' he

said contemptuously.

Ike went down to one of the saddles, removed the lariat and walked back with it. Old Caulfield's eyes were jumping from face to face – and to the lass rope. Over a long life he had seen death in many guises; he had accepted the Indian conviction that a hanged man lost his soul. Being shot was better; particularly in a fight.

Jered pulled Bryan to his feet from behind. The stocky man leaned to drop his smoke and stamp it out. Every eye was on him. He spun and lashed out, first with his right hand then with his other fist. He caught Jered standing too close and connected both times. Jered dropped like a stone.

Bryan whirled. Ike had his six-gun out and pointing. Bryan sneered. 'If you yank the trigger, you'll have more trouble than you can handle. My friends at the house is already nervous as cats.'

Ike marvelled at the man's seeming lack of fear. He said, 'I'm not goin' to shoot you, Mister Bryan, I'm goin' to whittle you down to size.'

Ike holstered the six-gun, wagged a finger of warning at old Caulfield, then began walking. Bryan had given proof he was no coward. He was built like a brick outhouse, clearly over the years had got into enough brawls to be confident.

He raised both arms and waited. Ike shuffled slightly to one side. Bryan shifted to this new direction. Ike did the same again; he shuffled to the right forcing Bryan to move again.

Old Caulfield was fascinated. He watched every move from a stump.

Bryan wearied of Ike's forcing and fading,

moving from side to side. Bryan was a brawler. If he knew much about manoeuvering during a fight he failed to demonstrate it. He had sized the constable up as a wiry, rock-fisted man, but too lean and light to be very dangerous.

Ike said, 'This is your chance, Mister Bryan. You better win before my partner comes around. He'll cut your throat.'

Bryan said nothing and acted as though he had not heard. He had taken the constable's measure, thought he was facing someone who was experienced enough to try to keep Bryan off balance by making him constantly shift his footing.

He was right, Ike was experienced. No cow town lawman still wearing a badge wasn't experienced, but Ike had another attribute; he didn't lose his temper in a brawl.

He had learned that early on. He had seen some very powerful men get stung into a fury. They almost always wound up badly beaten.

Old Caulfield, already disgusted, growled, 'You boys goin' to slow dance or fight?'

Bryan was distracted by the growl from behind. Only for a second or two. Ike moved one step and swung from the shoulder. Bryan's hat flew, his head snapped and his knees sagged. He had a bull-neck and a thick skull. Instinct told him to back-peddle. Ike missed the next strike. Bryan, dazed but seasoned, again acted from instinct. He ducked low and spun away making the constable miss his next strike.

Ike dropped his arms, watched Bryan's recovery, and smiled. When the renegade backed far enough to gain more time, he came out of a crouch fists poised as he moved obliquely, stalking the constable. This time it was Ike who had to shift his stance. As he was doing this Bryan came at him like a charging bull. He hit Ike in the ribs, forcing the lawman to give ground. He never slackened his onslaught.

Old Caulfield became excited. 'Harder,' he exclaimed. 'Keep at him.'

Jered sat up sucking air. He watched the fight, got a little unsteadily to his feet, moved toward the old man, caught him by the neck from behind with one huge hand and squeezed. Caulfield tried to break away, the big hand tightened. Caulfield jumped up. Jered held him at arm's length like a flopping chicken, yanked the old man close and slapped him hard across the face, then let the old man fall.

Bryan was pushing his advantage hard. He had Ike stumbling to avoid rock-like fists at the end of powerful arms. When Ike stopped to get his feet set, Bryan came in for the kill and ran head-first into a fist.

As before his head snapped, his knees loosened. Ike had been hurt but not badly enough, he leaned toward the stunned renegade, hit him twice, once on the slant of the jaw, the second time, as Bryan was going down, on the forehead.

It was over. Old Caulfield got back on his stump and groaned. Jered ignored him. 'I'll get the rope,' he said. 'You should've let me have him, Sheriff.'

The constable had a split lip from which he wiped blood on a filthy cuff as he watched the tall man retrieve the lariat. He went to lean above the downed renegade. Bryan looked up from eyes that did not quite focus. When Ike grabbed cloth to raise the outlaw, Bryan came up limp so Ike held him until Jered returned. Old Caulfield was still on his stump. As Jered yanked him off it the old man said, 'They'll be comin' directly.'

He was probably correct; the sun was rising, there was still a chill but it would dissipate within about an hour.

They took both prisoners to a pine with several thick low limbs. Without a word they gagged John Bryan, who was still recovering, lashed both hands behind his back using the renegade's bandana handkerchief, positioned him beneath a limb, Jered flung the rope over, Ike adjusted the slip-knot end, and John Bryan's mind finally cleared.

He tried to say something. As Ike was adjusting the hand-rope Bryan's eyes bulged, a vein in the side of his neck swelled. He tried to yell, sound came out muffled and hoarse.

He tried to move away. Jered yanked the rope taut. Bryan sounded as though he were choking. Ike got slack in the noose and re-positioned him. Jered yanked Bryan's trouser-belt free and knelt to bind the man's ankles. Bryan lashed out, barely missed the saloonman, who got behind him, encircled both legs and leaned all his weight into tightening the belt. This time when Bryan fought, he would have fallen if Ike hadn't caught him, steadied him and told him not to move.

Old Caulfield's normally ruddy complexion was

pale. He neither moved nor spoke. Another man, in his situation would have run; Caulfield seemed unable to run, he seemed to have taken root.

Ike took two dallies around the tree trunk, told Jered in a calm voice to boost Bryan off the ground. Again the frantic renegade bucked and arched, swung sideways and tried to bunch his knees to knock the tall man away.

Jered avoided the knees, took down a deep breath, looked John Bryan straight in the eyes as he leaned, encircled the straining, struggling outlaw around the waist and reared back.

Bryan was heavy. The tall man had to grunt and strain to lift the renegade a foot off the ground. Ike took up the slack around the tree. Jered's face was red from straining. He had John Bryan about two feet off the ground and could get him no higher when Ike said, 'High enough.'

Jered stepped away sucking air, his heart was pounding. A man hung properly from a decent height had his neck broken by the fall; this kind of hanging resulted in death from strangulation, which was not a very fast process.

Even after Bryan lost consciousness his body continued to twist and strain. Old Caulfield did not blink nor seem to be breathing as he watched the life slowly leave Bryan's body, and even afterwards when the body continued to jerk, twist and strain.

Ike made the rope fast, jerked his head toward the old man and started walking back out of the timber. He avoided looking at the twisting, turning body. Jered got the old man moving. They were now in full daylight with open country between themselves and the log house.

The horses had stood lined up like cows on a fence watching the hanging, which was fortunate because a man came out of the house, cleared his pipes, lustily expectorated and turned as two other men came out. They stood for a moment looking at the huge dead bear with the large steel trap on one foot. One man said, 'He must've got the old man down in the gully.'

The man behind him said, 'He lived long enough ... Where's John?'

'Taking care of his morning business, most likely.'

'We got to get along,' the other man said. He was wiry, tough, with thinning hair which showed when he raised his hat to scratch. He wore an ivory-stocked Colt.

The third man said, 'Ain't you goin' to look for him, Port? He was your blood kin.'

The wiry, balding man gave another cold answer to the question. 'If the bear got him all we'll find is guts strung out for a hunnert feet ... Let's get mounted.'

Ike, Jered and old Caulfield heard every word. The old man's lips moved without sound as Jered grabbed him, shoved him ahead closer to the curious horses, which hid them. They got too close, the horses inched warily away. Ike dropped flat palming his six-gun. Jered also went down, but the old man only knelt. He was glaring from pale eyes at the oncoming men, particularly at the one called Port who wore the ivory-stocked handgun.

Jered raised up, caught the old man by the scruff

of the neck and slammed him down, hard. He whispered. 'Not a sound, you old screwt. Not a sound an' don't move.'

Old Caulfield hissed back. 'Like shootin' fish in a rain barrel. Give me a gun; I'll kill that son of a bitch. All I've done for him an' he wouldn't even go see if the bear got me. I'll ...'

Jered hit the old man and snarled at him to be quiet. Caulfield fell silent but the look he put upon his nephew was deadly. He had both fists clenched against the ground.

The leading renegade suddenly halted. The horses had split up, he was staring up where daylight showed among the stumps and trees. Ike clearly heard him say, 'Jeez'chriz!' He pointed. The other renegades saw the body slowly twisting first to the right then to the left. Caulfield looked at the man beside him. 'Now,' he hissed. 'Shoot – *now, dammit!*'

This time he didn't whisper. His voice carried easily to the stiff-standing renegades. Stunned though they had been at the sight of their companion slowly turning at the end of a hang-rope, their instinctive reaction to the old man's voice was to whirl in a rush back to the log house. Old Caulfield was beside himself. He raised up like a lizard, front arms holding most of his body off the ground. He glared at Ike, 'You damned idiot! You stupid fool! You went an' let 'em escape.'

Jered reached, punched the old man flat as he said, 'They ain't goin' to escape. Calm down an' shut up.'

Caulfield was furious. He got back flat down but he didn't shut up. He hissed at Jered. 'What's the matter with you damned fools? Now they're forted up. There's plenty of grub. They can out-wait you if it takes a month.'

Ike reached to pat the old man's shoulder. 'There was five. Now there's three. You just relax and be patient.'

There was a small, narrow window in the north wall of the house. It was too high for even a tall man to see out of, but someone on a chair could scan straight ahead, but not very far on either side.

Ike braced his six-gun against a closed fist and fired. The window covering, which was rawhide scraped paper-thin to allow sunlight inside, blew apart and somewhere beyond it inside the slug struck an iron pot.

Ike sprang up. Jered grabbed the old man. They raced back to the timber with Jered practically carrying old Caulfield who kicked and swore and swung his arms.

When they had tree-shelter Jered released the old man, who turned and made a wild swing that missed the tall man by a foot. Jered leaned, grabbed a fistful of shirt, yanked the old man close, half off the ground and said, 'You try that once more an' we won't bother takin' you along.' He released the old man with a shove. 'How long you figure it's goin' to take your nephew to suspicion you helped us?'

Old Caulfield had to fight to hold his balance. When he was able he stared at the saloonman without speaking.

There was heat, less troublesome among the trees than beyond them but enough to inspire thirst. Ike asked the old man where the nearest creek was. Caulfield answered sullenly. 'Ain't no crick within two miles … But there's a sump-spring; I'll show you.'

Jered grabbed the old man. 'How far, you old goat?'

Caulfield raised a thin arm. 'Hundred feet. You want me to show you or not?'

He was right. The spring had been cleared and rocked around a small pool. The old man stood back to watch his captors drink. He had a skinning knife scabbarded in his right hand boot. They were belly down in front of him drinking. He waited until they pulled back then went ahead to also drink.

He hadn't made the attempt for a practical reason. His kind was never confused, they figured odds and angles. After what he had heard his nephew say about him, Caulfield simply changed sides, which did not mean he approved of his companions, it meant he now wanted them to kill his nephew because he couldn't, he only had the boot-knife, which was as useless as tits on a man under the present circumstances.

As he arose flinging off water he eyed the tall man and the constable. 'This here is where I get my water. I don't know what you two figure to do, but I'll tell you one thing; they got enough grub to last them a month – but I only fetched in two buckets of water yestiddy, so if you figure to starve them out … For the damned life of me I can't figure out why you didn't kill all three of them ... Hell, they was easy targets.' The old man spat. His anger had turned to solid disgust. 'You're crazy,' he said in summation, and went to sit on a rock.

Jered said, 'You got a cache, Mister Caulfield?'

The old man's faded pale eyes lifted. 'You ever know anyone livin' in this high country that didn't have a cache against four foot of snow – *Mister* Whatever-your-name-is?'

Jered's amusement barely showed. 'No, I never did ... where is it?'

'Back yonder on a platform high in an old fir tree.'

'How far back, Mister Caulfield?'

'Not awful far. Maybe quarter of a mile. If you ever lived in this kind of country, *Mister* beanpole, you'd know not to make it any farther than you can hear, because varmints that climb can scent it up, an' in winter them as can't climb like wolves, try for it ... That damned old black bear ... He's raided my cache two years straight runnin'. That's why I sat out to trap him. He's wise, I'll tell you for a fact. He knew where I lived. He never made a sound when he climbed that tree ... When he was through there wasn't enough left to feed a badger. Not only that but I had to re-build the platform. I wanted that bear dead as bad as I want my nephew dead ... I got the bear.'

The old man showed a merciless smile.

Jered and Ike exchanged looks before Ike said, 'Mister Caulfield, it's likely to take some time waitin' out your friends, Jered an' I, an' you too, are likely to get hungry before this is over.'

The old man spat his words. 'My friends! I didn't want them to show up. I like livin' my own way. They rode in and got settled. Wasn't nothin' I could do. Their kind'll kill you just for target practice. Friends! I wish the lot of you was in hell an' I could get on with my life.'

Jered waited out the anger before speaking. 'You go back, get some grub from your cache an' we'll wait here for you to come back ... Be sure you come back, Mister Caulfield. I can track you over a glass window an' there are still some lass ropes down yonder.'

The old man sat a long time in sullen silence before arising and hiking off through the timber. Ike said, 'I wouldn't bet a plugged cartwheel the old bastard won't keep right on going.'

Jered shrugged and turned to look in the direction of the log house. 'If he does I'll track him to where we can leave him hangin' in a tree.' All the same Jered got tiredly to his feet and followed the old man.

Ike ached all over, his face was swollen, his lips were scabbing over, his eyes felt as though they had sand in them, he was also very hungry.

He leaned against a tree and chewed a dead cigar while watching the log house. For a damned fact there had to be an easier way to serve the Lord than being a lawman.

8

A Long Day

Ike wondered what the renegades were doing in
the log house. He knew what they *weren't* doing —
peeking out that high, narrow window.

They had their outfits inside with them, which
meant extra ammunition, and that was an
advantage. Ike and the saloonman had only the
loads in their shellbelts and the chambers of their
Winchesters.

He and Jered were not only out-gunned, they
were afoot. They were also in the open, but there
was good cover as long as they remained among
the trees.

Water, Ike decided. How this was going to end
would depend on water. The lack of it in the cabin
might just off-set the disadvantage of fewer bullets
as well as being out-numbered.

Being out-numbered did not bother the constable very much. Most of his work wearing a badge
had been concluded without support. Interesting
thing about people; they raised hell and propped it

up when trouble came, then ducked for cover and remained there leaving things up to their law officer.

He decided behind a prodigious yawn that if he got back to Cedarton he was going to eat three medium steaks, drink a potful of black java, clean up at the barber's bath-house out back, then sleep for a solid week.

The sun climbed, shadows moved among the trees, Jered and the old man returned with food, and someone down at the house slid something heavy across the rough wooden floor.

Old Caulfield sniffed. 'Pilin' my furniture against the door. Mighty brave; they're protected, they got guns, an' they're scairt of two smelly scarecrows.'

The food consisted of dry berries as hard as rocks, jerky cured to perfection, pine nuts which had been roasted, and something Ike thought was shrivelled, de-hydrated potatoes which turned out to be wild onions strong enough to stand without help.

Jered ate watching the house. His first mouthful of the dried 'potatoes' made water spring to his eyes. He fled to the rocked-up spring. The old man snorted. 'Town folks got no guts,' he told Ike. 'Them tubers'll rid a man of worms, clean out his bile and make a man regular.'

Ike ate slowly. Short of getting the renegades out of their fort by thirst, which might take several days, there had to be something else to be done. He did not cotton to the notion of waiting up here one minute longer than he had to. Besides, old Caulfield was beginning to get on his nerves.

He asked if the old man had any blasting powder,

which was a normal question; in this kind of rough country men usually kept a few sticks around.

But not old Caulfield. 'What'n hell would I keep dynamite for? I ain't no rock miner. An' I've known fellers to get blown to smithereens.'

Jered returned breathing better but still with watery eyes. He sank down next to the old man and glared. Caulfield cackled. 'When I was your age, sonny, men ate them things by the handful three times a day. Kept them regular an' all.'

Jered growled his reply. 'An' now they're all dead … Shut up, you old goat. Just shut up for a while. You got a tongue that hinges in the middle. *Keep quiet!*'

Ike went to the rock-spring, drank, held his feverish face in cold water for a while, sat up letting daytime warmth dry him off, eventually returned to the timber where the old man and Jered were acting as though neither of the other one existed.

Jered had a chew in his cheek. He spat, waited until Ike sat down then said, 'Old flannel-mouth here's got a root cellar dug under his house.'

Ike raised his eyebrows. 'Is there a way out of it, Caulfield?'

'No, there's no door out. Whoever heard of diggin' a root cellar with a door out of it? That's the trouble with you town folks; don't have a lick of sense about how other folks live. Only way in an' out is through the floor.'

Jered reached almost casually and slapped the old man.

For fifteen minutes they sat in stony silence. Blue jays arrived overhead to squawk and spring among the topmost limbs looking down. They called back and forth about the two-legged things on the ground below. They also scolded the two-legged things.

Anyone who spent much time in high country learned to listen to blue jays; they were forest sentinels, anything out of the ordinary, such as people, would draw them to scold and make enough warning noises to be heard a mile.

Old Caulfield glared venomously overhead. He'd had an on-going feud with blue jays for almost forty years. They had ruined a hundred careful stalks when he'd been after camp meat. If bullets hadn't been so hard to come by and so expensive there wouldn't have been a blue jay within a mile of his stump ranch.

The birds never completely abandoned their noisy outrage but most of them left the area. Caulfield's lips moved but he did not make a sound. He despised those warning-birds above all other critters, even bears and catamounts.

Ike was snoring. Jered ejected his cud and tipped down his hat, but he did not sleep, he alternately watched the log house and the old screwt who had built it.

Ike got his rest, the sun was sliding away, acquiring a rusty look as it did so, and old Caulfield was sleeping like a log when Jered quietly spoke from below his tipped forward hat.

'There's somethin' goin' on at the house.'

Ike rubbed his eyes, spat, scratched inside his shirt and looked southward. He saw nothing and heard nothing. The old man slept on. They

ignored him; he was still their captive but they
viewed him more as a nuisance. He had made it
clear he strongly resented the intruders, both
inside his house and outside it.

Ike was yawning when he saw something move
rapidly past the narrow high window. By the time
he had quit yawning it was gone. Without looking
away from the house he said, 'What can they do in
broad daylight?'

Jered's reply was practical. 'Nothin'. But they
can't stay in there without water, an' the night's
dark.'

Ike leaned back watching the house. Behind
them the stiffening corpse was motionless. It was in
full view of the forted-up renegades.

The old man choked, sat up clearing his pipes
and coughed. Neither of his companions paid him
any attention. He addressed Jered. 'Can you spare
a mite off your plug? I run out of eatin' tobacco six,
seven months ago.'

Jered fished forth his plug, tossed it to the old
man caught it when the old man tossed it back and
pocketed it, all without a word.

Caulfield settled the cud and sighed. When next
he spoke he sounded almost civil. 'You boys got no
idea how a man misses the simple pleasures, livin'
far out.'

They ignored him.

In his better mood he did not appear to notice.
'They got a choice, ain't they? Bust out shootin' an'
runnin', or wait until dark and try to sneak away …
My idea'd be to slip down closer after sunset …
When they make their run for it shoot 'em like

varmints.'

Jered slowly faced the old man, held Caulfield's gaze for a moment then just as slowly turned away. Old Caulfield got red as a beet. His mellowed mood vanished. His shrill, indignant voice was too loud for his captors as he said, 'Yeah; you town fellers know it all, don't you? I'll tell you —'

Jered leaned and swung his open hand. The sound was of a very distant gunshot. The old man's cud flew several feet and landed in the dirt. Caulfield leaned to retrieve it, brush it off and tuck it back into his cheek. Not until he had accomplished this did he raise a hand to his cheek and hiss at the saloonman. 'I'm goin' to pay you back, you long-legged sap sucker.'

Jered almost smiled at the old man. 'Keep your voice down or I'll wring your scrawny neck.'

The day wore along, the jay birds eventually departed, flies came close but would not go where the shadows were deepest. Jered went after a drink, returned and said, 'I favour goin' in after 'em if they don't come out.'

Ike ignored that. It was too risky and the saloonman knew it; he was talking out his frustration. Waiting was something Jered Salte had never been very good at.

Ike dozed again as the afternoon heat increased. When he awakened the sun was farther down and more rusty-coloured than pale. The horses were restless, whatever grass had been inside the corral had been eaten down to dust. There was also the matter of water. Horses needed water. Ike asked the old man why he hadn't ditched water from the rock-spring and got a reply he might have expected. 'Mostly I don't keep my horses in there. Only when I figure to use 'em.'

With nothing better to do Ike kept this discussion alive by saying, 'It'd only take maybe a day or two to bring water down here.'

Caulfield scowled. 'That ground's got rocks in it bigger'n I am.'

'You got time, Mister Caulfield. I never liked to see animals go thirsty or hungry.'

The old man did not respond. For once he elected not to argue.

Jered walked back through the trees as far as the cache and walked back. Ike understood but did not imitate his friend. Jered was restless, Constable Bowen had enough patience for both of them.

The sun balanced above the farthest rims, immense, glowing like copper and seemingly reluctant to continue its slide from sight.

Old Caulfield spoke. 'Fifteen, twenty minutes an' we can creep closer to the corral.'

His companions ignored what was obvious. Jered lifted out his handgun, turned the cylinder, took his Winchester into his lap, examined it too, then leaned the carbine aside and composed himself to watch the house.

Ike said, 'Call down there, Jered. Ain't much of a chance but they might come out.'

Jered's reply came in an inflectionless drawl. 'I don't want 'em to surrender. I keep thinkin' back to that unarmed old man doin' his chores, an' his wife face down wearin' her apron.'

Nothing more was said on this subject. Ike

chewed a stogie he had cut in half, but there was no more satisfaction this time than there had been before. He spat out the chewed cigar.

Jered had been watching. 'When we get done with this, you'd do well to buy some eatin' tobacco, it'll stand by you better'n somethin' you got to set fire to.'

Ike made no reply. He picked up his Winchester as he asked old Caulfield a question. 'How long have you lived up here?'

'More years than you are old,' came the waspish reply.

'How many times has your nephew come to visit?'

'Three, four times. He knows I don't need visitors but he comes anyway.'

'And pays you?'

'I don't deny that. Pays for horseshoes, whatever he needs like tinned grub. I can use the money. But I'd as lief he never come at all an' he knows it.'

Jered broke up this conversation. 'Someone looked out the window. There ... He's back.'

Whichever raider it was he had to be standing on a chair. The old man growled a name. 'That's my nephew ... Well, what you waitin' for? He's outlined in the window like a preacher.'

Neither Ike or Jered replied nor looked at the old man. This was the first they'd seen Porter Caulfield standing still. The outlaw called out.

'How much for you fellers to look the other way?'

Ike's answer was droll. 'Why? The old man told us you got a houseful of grub. Just stay comfortable in there an' wait us out.'

Caulfield's reply came back swiftly. 'Yeah, but we don't like bein' penned up ... How much?'

Ike's next reply was given in the same tone of voice. 'An' we don't like murderers.'

'Did you say you got my uncle with you?'

'Yep.'

There was a pause before the man at the window called again. 'We figured the bear got him, old damned fool goin' out at night to set a trap.'

Caulfield fairly danced with anger. Jered pointed a stiff warning finger without speaking. It worked as well as a verbal caution would have, the older man stopped his indignant posturing when Ike called to the cabin again.

'Caulfield, you're not leavin' this clearing standing up.'

'Who are you?'

'Constable down at Cedarton. Ike Bowen.'

Again there was an interlude of silence before the renegade spoke. It was just before the dialogue was resumed that Jered ripped out a hair-curling curse under his breath before saying, 'He's keepin' us occupied Ike. Watch the door. It looked to me like it was bein' eased open.'

Ike watched the door instead of the window but it was already beginning to get dark. If the door had been opened he could see no sign of it.

Jered was tense. 'We got to get closer.'

They took the old man with them, used every shadow they could find, every kind of cover including the hungry horses.

Caulfield moved as stealthily as his companions. For once he appeared to be as engrossed in what they were doing as were Ike and Jered.

The fading but still visible man at the narrow window called again. 'You got a price? We can meet it.'

None of the crawlers replied. He called again, sounding slightly less assured this time. 'We'll trade you a pouch of gold coins for the old man.'

Caulfield got no answer; the stalkers were no longer among the trees. The renegade would realise the moment Ike or Jered spoke that they were just beyond the corral, close to the house.

He made one last call. 'We got you out-numbered and out-gunned. It's up to you.'

Ike was sweating although the increasingly dusky evening was not all that warm. The old man was between the younger men. Jered raised his head to gesture. He would go around the corral to the west and take the old man with him. Ike nodded. Caulfield looked from one of them to the other. When Jered rapped him with his fist and jerked his head, the old man dutifully followed. He had already figured out that if one of his companions could get far enough around the corral to have a good sighting of the doorway while the other one remained where he could stop a rush for the horses, the stalkers just might succeed. One thing he knew for a fact, the constable and the saloonman were in this to the finish.

He and Jered belly-crawled. The horses watched their progress. Dusk thickened until it was hard for the old man to make out the animals. When Jered stopped Caulfield stopped. Of his two captors he liked the tall man the least, but right now his personal dislike was sublimated. He had come to the conclusion that his companions had better succeed, because his nephew and his friends would kill him out of hand.

Night came gradually, weak starlight aided by a thickening scimitar moon cast light poorly and weakly. The old man crawled close to Jered and whispered. 'They ain't foolish enough to try for the horses.'

Jered nodded, watching the door, which was not visible enough for him to be able to see anything beyond the slight recess in logs where it was located. He lifted out his six-gun and resumed crawling.

Now the horses were nervous; they moved, turned back, split off and milled together. Where Ike was waiting it was obvious if the men in the cabin could see at all, they would interpret the nervous horses correctly; the men who had left their companion hanging from a pine limb were crawling closer to the house, past the corral, otherwise the horses would not be acting spooky.

Ike got as close as he dared. Corral stringers were less than three feet from him. The animals were dividing their concern between two smelly creatures coming around the southwest side of the corral, and the single one farther back but creeping closer.

A horse snorted and Ike swore under his breath. It was so quiet that noise would surely reach through the open window.

It evidently did. The renegades became absolutely quiet.

Jered and Caulfield stopped moving. Gradually the horses began to lose interest in them. A horse's attention span was not great. Without an undeniable threat they generally lost interest.

But the horse who had snorted had spoiled whatever opportunity Ike and Jered might have had to nail the fleeing renegades the moment they broke clear and ran for it.

Although Jered and the old man could not see the door clearly, Ike could and it was tightly closed. Jered looked at the old man, who raised and lowered bony shoulders, leaned close and whispered. 'My nephew ain't kept alive this long by lettin' himself get ambushed. His kind can smell bad trouble a long way off ... They're goin' to set in there until morning.'

Jered relaxed against the ground. 'Maybe. You want a chew?'

The old man held up his claw of a hand. Jered placed the plug on his palm and waited to get it back before he also gnawed at a corner. 'That bear's goin' to start stinkin' by tomorrow. Look over there; he's swole as big as pumpkin.'

For once old Caulfield did not say a word.

9

Guns in the Night

Normally men as tired as the Cedarton duo had every right to be, would have slept through any attempt of the renegades to escape, which it seemed had been part of the plan of the outlaws.

They were quiet in the cabin. It required no particular savvy to figure out that their pursuers had to have kept in the saddle without rest for a long time.

It was sound reasoning but for overlooking the fact that their stalkers had used most of this day resting. Also, the renegades who attacked suddenly, fiercely then ran, were not convinced anyone would remain on their trail. They had out-run a number of possemen, and even more furious stockmen. Their trade required abrupt attacks and fast escapes.

But their major oversight had to do with the kind of men waiting out in the night. Neither the very tall man nor the town constable had considered abandoning the manhunt, nor would they have.

Old Caulfield sprawled flat beside Jered, who listened to the old man's even breathing as he watched the front of the house.

He liked the idea of only one door in the house. Whatever the old man's reason for not having an exit as well as an entrance, Jered was satisfied. If the old man had been asked he could have explained that with only one door, which could be barred from the inside, he could sleep without fear of being interrupted by strangers. That too was a good idea, except that his latest visitors hadn't come at night; they had arrived in daylight when the old man was doing his chores.

Ike wearied of waiting, crept inside the corral with horses watching. He moved without haste toward the opposite stringers, had almost reached them when a horse snorted and shied.

He looked around. The damned animal had been one of the old man's sorrels. His attention was drawn forward by a faint scraping sound which was so faint that in daylight he probably would not have heard it.

With difficulty he made out a head and shoulders in the window. Because he was flat with moving animals passing and re-passing, he doubted that the watcher could have made him out, but for a blessed fact unless the watcher was simple in the head he would know exactly what someone was doing in the corral.

The vague outline disappeared. Ike reached the southernmost corral stringers, lifted out his Colt and waited. Even simpletons would realise that if someone set their saddle stock free, they would have about the same chance of escaping as a snowball in hell.

He tightened his grip on the weapon and waited. To his right somewhere Jered would be waiting too. Old Caulfield didn't much matter. If Ike had known the old screwt was sound asleep he would have approved.

For the outlaws, the idea of waiting for the wee hours to escape was clearly not going to work. Someone was near the corral, which would have been their objective; they needed their horses to get away on. With someone who had understood that, waiting for them to make the attempt, the opportunity was no longer feasible.

They lost the thin edge of complacency they'd held to since they knew enemies were stalking them. One outlaw, with light reddish hair and pale blue eyes, sat on the floor. He was thirsty; there was little water left in the old man's buckets because with the sun beating down on the cabin roof all day, they had replaced sweat about as fast as it appeared.

The pale-eyed man regarded his companions and said, 'Water's about gone, they're between us an' the horses … How many are out there?'

Port Caulfield answered curtly. 'That don't matter. We got ourselves boxed in.'

The pale-eyed man flared back. 'It *does* matter! If it's a posse we're bad off. If it's just –'

'Shut up,' Port Caulfield said. 'We got to get out of here while it's still dark.'

The pale-eyed man arose, went to stand below the window making no attempt to stand on the chair. 'We should've fought it out when John was with us.' He turned. 'Port, if we get out of here we'll be on foot. They'll have the horses.'

Caulfield raised his hat, scratched his balding head and said, 'Right now we got to figure a way to slip away with them watchin'.'

'An' how do we do that? There's only one door; they know that by now ... Port; we got to talk our way out of here. There ain't no other way.'

Caulfield put a scalding stare upon the speaker which was not visible in darkness but the coldness of his voice matched the look. 'Talk our way out? Didn't you see John hangin' from that tree – you damned fool. They'd let us come out walkin' then kill us where we stand. Whoever they are, take my word for it, they want blood.'

Desperation being the parent of despair, the renegades said no more. Time passed, cold air came through the lightless window, they paced like caged animals. The pale-eyed man returned to the chair gazing up at the narrow window. 'There ain't no other way,' he said softly, as though speaking to himself, and climbed atop the chair.

The horses were milling. He watched for a moment then climbed back down to say, 'Port, they're closin' around us.'

The wiry man made a sarcastic reply. 'What did you expect? They've had all day.'

'Port. It's a slim chance but we got to try'n talk our way out.'

Caulfield snorted, went to a chair and sat down, hitched at his holster to get it hanging free and was quiet for a long time. It was gall but there it was;

their fort had become their prison. He said, 'Son of a bitch!' and shot up to his feet glaring. 'Try the door, just a crack. If one's close enough to see we can whittle down the odds.'

The pale-eyed man did not move. 'Time's past for guns, Port.'

'They'll shoot you down like a dog when you step outside.'

'An' if we shoot one of them – then what? At least we got a chance if we talk.' The pale-eyed man added something else. 'One of us calls from the doorway. When they come to talk ...' He patted his holster. 'That's what I meant when I said we got to talk, got to get them close enough to see.'

Caulfield stood gazing at the shadowy man some distance from him. He hadn't understood, he had thought the pale-eyed man meant to surrender and he would never have done that – better to die fighting if a man was going to die anyway.

Caulfield said, 'Try it. You call to 'em an' I'll crack the door to see if they're listenin'.'

'Don't use your gun,' the pale-eyed man said as he went to the chair and climbed atop it. He came up very slowly. At the same time his head appeared he called into the hushed, dark, chilly night.

'We want to palaver. No guns, just palaver.'

The night remained silent. He craned to see what the horses were acting uneasy about, saw nothing but peeled logs and milling horses and tried again. 'This here condition can last a long time. We don't figure you want that an' neither do we.'

He waited, but again there was no response, no sound at all from the area of the corral.

He tried one more time. 'We got plenty of money. Enough for you fellers to set back a long time.'

There was no reply to this either. Below, the balding man who wore a holstered Colt with ivory handles tugged at the britches of the man on the chair as he hissed, 'Get down. They ain't goin' to give an inch. I told you that. Get down.'

The pale-eyed man got off the chair. He and Porter Caulfield stared at each other. Before either of them could speak a slightly raised calm voice called out. 'It won't last a long time. Maybe one more day, then you bastards will be drinkin' your own sweat. The old man told us how much water you got.' There was a pause then the same calm voice continued. 'You want to palaver? We don't … You come out of there with your arms over your heads an' stop in front of the door.'

Caulfield replied in scorn. 'You want us, come get us.'

This time a second voice called out. It came from east of the corrals. 'That's what we figure to do. Me, personally, I don't want you to come out with your hands up … But you can come out if you want to.'

Caulfield returned to his chair. He was a merciless, deadly individual who had eluded many pursuers. He was a renegade with confidence. Once, an old black woman he and his raiders had let live as she stood over her dead husband and the ranchers they had worked for, had looked Caulfield in the eye as he sat his horse with a smoking gun. 'You goin' to die a bad death. You got 'em both against you. Him an' the Devil. No man ever overcome them odds. One or the other'll kill you an' I hope he does it real slow. Mister, you're ridin' straight to hell.'

Caulfield would have shot her too but one of his killers had seen a band of men riding hard toward the raided ranch.

He had led the flight on fresh animals. The pursuers hadn't even got close.

Until he was sitting in the dark he had not thought back to what the old black woman had said. He didn't think about it now except fleetingly before he arose from the chair.

'All right,' he growled. 'They want a fight an' we got no choice, so we'll give 'em one.'

The pale-eyed man crossed to the door, leaned to listen and straightened up saying, 'It'll be like runnin' a gauntlet … Even if we reach the gully they'll be hard after us … Port?'

Caulfield spoke coldly. 'You got another idea, Pat?'

Instead of answering the pale-eyed man listened at the door again, then gripped the latch, squeezed and as the hanger came out of its deep notch he eased the door inward by inches, soundlessly and slowly.

Nothing happened. To the men in the house this was more ominous than if something had happened. Whoever they were, they were out there waiting.

The door came back another six inches. The pale-eyed man and Caulfield exchanged looks. Caulfield palmed his six-gun as he stared at the other man. 'Shoot toward the corral,' he said. 'That'll get the horses to runnin' wild. That's about all we can do. Run for the damned arroyo an' don't stop. *Open it!*'

The pale-eyed man drew his six-gun with his right hand and pulled the door wide with his left hand. Nothing happened. Caulfield said, 'Gawddammit,' and sprang forward.

The fleeing renegades blew the night apart with gun thunder, muzzle blasts of red fire marked their racing progress. They were passing the dead bear when two hand guns fired in their direction. One shot ripped the bear open, gas whistled from the swollen carcass. Caulfield paused two seconds to fire at the flame of that unseen gunman then raced ahead. He was nearing the arroyo when another shot came from the south side of the corral where horses were racing in terror, so close that Ike had to scramble between stringers to avoid being trampled. The renegades had done a good job of stampeding the animals. If the old man hadn't put a lot of time and work into building corrals strong enough to withstand this kind of abuse the terror-stricken horses would have broken loose.

Jered fired three more times. One of the fleeing men went down in a writhing heap. Incredibly, he was the only outlaw who was hit.

There were of course reasons. One, it was dark. Two, fleeing men running apart were difficult targets, and for Ike who'd had to scramble out of the corral and therefore had been momentarily unable to use his gun, the time he'd lost before he could fire again aided the escape, but mostly it was the darkness.

Jered was on his feet running toward the arroyo before Ike saw him, sprang up and followed. Far behind them old Caulfield, with no real interest in the fight, went to his log house, stood gazing at the wreckage, and instead of swearing, sat on a chair and groaned aloud.

Someone just below the lip of the arroyo was waiting. When Jered ran up the sniper fired, spun Jered by impact then raced southward in the darkness.

When Ike came up the tall man was trying to tie off the bleeding from his left upper arm with a bandana and was not having much luck. Ike leathered his weapon, tied the wound so tight the bleeding stopped, then asked Jered if he had got the man who had winged him.

Instead of replying Jered went to the edge of the crumbly bank and went sliding toward the gully below. Dirt, dust, even some rocks followed him down.

Ike did the same, landed on his feet where Jered had a finger to his lips. They could distinctly hear someone racing desperately southward.

Ike turned to the tall man, 'Get a couple of horses. I'll follow them on foot.'

Ike did not look back. If he had he would have seen the tall man standing where Ike had left him, unwilling for a while to go back for horses. But he eventually did, by which time the cold was especially noticeable and there was no sign of old Caulfield.

Jered was saddling two horses one-handedly,

which was difficult but not impossible, although bridling them was definitely a two-handed undertaking, when the old man came shuffling from his house to shove Jered out of the way, bridle the horses and hand Jered the reins. Until then old Caulfield did not see the bandaged, bloody arm. He said, 'I'll saddle up,' and moved toward one of his sorrels, but Jered did not wait.

The excited saddle animal did not wait to be gigged into covering the distance to that game trail leading down into the arroyo, in fact he would have plunged down the trail if Jered hadn't hauled him back. He might have made it, then again in the dark he might have gone over the edge.

The old man lost sight of Jered as he led his mount out of the corral, stiffly climbed aboard and walked his horse without haste past the bear toward the edge of the arroyo, and halted dead still at the sight of a man sitting up, grimacing in pain.

The old man dismounted, looked for the gun he knew would be somewhere close by, found it, shoved it down his britches and finally approached the injured man whose jaws were locked against waves of pain.

The old man stood gazing at the renegade for a moment before leaning to hoist him to his feet. He trailed his horse behind as he helped the injured man back to his cabin where he sat him on a chair, went back to care for his horse, turned all the horses loose and returned to the cabin. Old Caulfield leaned in his doorway gazing dispassionately at the wounded renegade, who asked if the old man had any laudanum.

Caulfield shook his head. 'Where was you hit?'

The renegade put a hand to his left thigh where it was difficult to see bleeding in the dark. The old man lighted one of his lamps, held it low to inspect the wound and snorted. 'That ain't no more'n a graze.' He stepped away to place the lamp on a table as he also said, 'Sonny, I been hurt worse'n that an' never even quit talkin'.'

The old man faced around. 'They're goin' to hang you when they get back.'

The outlaw was not listening, he was trying to determine if he was still bleeding. He was. 'Give me some rags,' he said.

The old man didn't move. 'It'll quit bleedin' by itself in a little while.'

'Some rags, you damned old bastard.'

Caulfield slowly lifted out the renegade's gun, aimed and cocked it. For ten seconds they looked at each other. The outlaw had forgotten his wound.

'Boot's on the other foot now,' Caulfield said. 'An' you're a whisker away from gettin' gut-shot. That'll give you somethin' to really groan about – you bastard.'

The outlaw neither spoke nor moved. He was in pain. He was also convinced the old man would kill him. He finally spoke in a different tone of voice. 'Mister Caulfield, it wasn't me that said we should come up here an' move in on you.'

'I know that – you bastard. It was Port. Now tell me that lawman and his beanpole-friend don't have good reason to kill the lot of you.'

'I held the horses is all, Mister Caulfield.'

The old man snorted. 'All of a sudden the

world's full of fellers who just held the horses.' His finger tightened inside the trigger guard but it was too dark for the wounded man to notice.

'I'm bleedin' to death, Mister Caulfield. F'chrissake help me stop the bleedin'.'

Caulfield eased down the dog, holstered the revolver and went about setting up chairs, tidying up by puny lamplight and eventually fired up his old stove with the coffee pot atop it. He closed the door to keep cold out but there was nothing he could do about the shattered rawhide at the window.

Every now and then he would halt and cock his head. There were no gunshots. He growled at the wall, 'They're gettin' away. I told them idiots to shoot. It would have ended yestiddy. But no, they wanted you bastards alive.' He turned. 'Ain't you bled to death yet – you bastard?'

10

A Surprise

The old man's prisoner was the outlaw Terry Bligh, the least noticeable, most nondescript of the Caulfield raiders. His companions considered him to have been born with one foot out of the stirrup. But he was dependable. He was also an off-hand killer.

The old man asked who had escaped. His prisoner replied in a dull voice. 'Two, your nephew and Pat Ruggles.' He stopped stuffing a soiled bandana inside his torn britches where bleeding was subsiding. 'There was another feller. We left him miles back because he couldn't ride no farther.'

The old man was not interested. He moved around putting his house to rights and muttering grisly threats as he did this.

One distant gunshot echoed down the cold pre-dawn. The old man stopped, cocked his head for the next shot, but there was none, and that increased his crankiness. 'Somebody got shot.

Question is – who?'

Bligh had finished making his impromptu bandage and was wiping blood on his trousers when he said, 'One shot could be a miss.'

The old man went back to his work without speaking. The more wreckage he cleaned up the more his temper rose. When he turned back for some coffee he said, 'I ought to blow your damned head off. Look at this place. You got any idea how long it took me to make that table an' them chairs?'

Bligh watched old Caulfield draw off a cup of coffee, looking hopeful. The old man remained where the heat was watching his prisoner from an expressionless face. Bligh asked for coffee. Caulfield crossed the room and flung the cup's contents into the face of the wounded man.

Bligh squawked, started to jump up, pain lanced through him like fire. He sank down mopping coffee off with a filthy sleeve. He made no threat, in fact he said nothing, but the look on his face was deadly.

The old man went back for a re-fill. There was another gunshot, closer this time. What bothered him was that this gunshot had sounded as though whoever had fired it was returning to the clearing. He finished his java, went to the door, leaned to look out, saw nothing but the dead bear, slowly closed and barred the door from the inside, and worried.

Dawn was breaking, the chill outside was sharp, inside the house was warm. Terry Bligh's mood was deteriorating. In a sour voice he said, 'I don't suppose you got any whiskey?'

The old man went to a box over his wall-bunk, took down a bottle looking both surprised and pleased. As he turned he said, 'You'n your friends missed it.'

Bligh did not reply.

Caulfield took down two swallows, considered his prisoner, went over and handed him the bottle. As Bligh was drinking Caulfield said, 'Take all you want. When them lads get back to hang you it'll be easier if you're smoked to the gills.'

Bligh handed back the bottle, coughed and pushed away water that had sprung from his eyes. 'What in the hell is in that stuff, Mister Caulfield?'

'Oh. Now it's *Mister* Caulfield, is it?' He did not answer the question about the whiskey, but took another swallow and returned the bottle to its hiding place.

Outside, they heard horses. The old man's anxiety increased, but he concealed it from Terry Bligh, who was beginning to look hopeful as the old man went to the chair below the window, climbed up, looked out and breathed a grateful curse. 'It's the loose-stock, they come back. They're out by the corral.' He climbed off the chair. 'Liked to give me a worry for a spell, there.'

Terry Bligh's injury had become more painful than dangerous. His entire hip was swelling but the bleeding was down to an occasional drop or two. Between loss of blood and whiskey he felt an increasing drowsiness. With an effort he arose, crossed lamely to the wall bunk, eased carefully down, stifled a howl when he raised both legs, lay back and looked at Caulfield.

The old man nodded. 'Get some practice, partner. Lyin' like that's how you're goin' to spend eternity.'

Bligh's drowsiness increased until he could not keep his eyes open. The old man ignored the bunk, cracked the door a few inches and peered out. It was light enough to see the bear distinctly. The horses had evidently tanked up at his water hole, had grazed their fill and were now standing like statues waiting for the sun to warm them on the north side of the corrals, beyond which was the stiff-hanging corpse of John Bryan.

He heard a slight sound southward and swung his head. It had come from down in the arroyo. He eased back, barred the door, yanked the shellbelt from slumbering Terry Bligh, hung it around his own spare middle, went after his scattergun, wrapped in an old hide beside some carelessly-piled Indian blankets, searched for the gun's shells, did not find them and had to be content with the two loads in the old shotgun. They might be all he'd need, depending on who was out there and how close they got.

There was no more noise for a long time. Caulfield's nerves were crawling. He had survived a number of stalks by bloody-hand Indians but that had been long ago. Since his youth he hadn't felt threatened more than a few times, usually by bears or catamounts, but the cold up his backbone returned from over the years exactly as he had felt it decades earlier.

He started when Terry Bligh began snoring. He glared toward the bunk, crossed toward it, rolled the wounded man onto his side and the snoring stopped. He stood a moment looking down. No matter how much whiskey he might have downed he never would have been able to sleep if he'd been in the renegade's boots.

He got more coffee. He should have been hungry. Under less troublesome circumstances he would have been. Right now he knew for a blessed fact someone was outside. The question was – who?

The early day was utterly still – and cold. Foraging critters might be up yonder among the trees but at the house and clearing there was not a sound, not even from the motionless horses who were being slowly warmed by fresh sunlight.

The old man lifted out Bligh's gun and examined it. The weapon was old, there was no trace of its original bluing, but it was in good shape and fully loaded with a cylinder that did not make a sound when it was turned. Evidently its owner was a rarity among renegades, he kept his shooting iron in excellent shape with oil, rubbing, and good handling.

Caulfield crossed to the barred door, put his ear against it, thought he heard voices, leaned harder, heard nothing and remained in place listening. He would have bet his best horse he had heard voices. They seemed to be north of the house. He scuttled to the window, climbed onto the chair and peeked out.

He didn't see anyone but the sun-absorbing horses had their heads up, their ears pointing. He watched them; horses were curious and wary animals. It did not have to mean their attention had been attracted by men, it could have been that as the sun rose, dead bear scent carried northward to them. One thing was a dead-sure cinch, by the time the sun got directly overhead that bear was going to be wafting his odour far and wide.

At this moment Caulfield did not think of something that might have made him cuss a blue streak later: Somehow he was going to have to drag that damned bear far away, and since neither of his sorrel horses could be chummed into helping, the chore would be up to the old man.

He got down from the window. Bligh was snoring on his back again. The old man went over to roll him onto his side again, this time roughly enough for the wounded man to groan in his sleep. His gunshot-graze was now swollen so much it was putting considerable pressure on his bloody, torn britches.

Bligh looked like the wrath of gawd. He was filthy, unshaven, sunken-eyed with pale lips and unkempt hair.

Caulfield went to his water bucket. The dipper was resting on the dry bottom. He did not swear, he simply sank down on a chair. He had been a trapper, a professional hunter, occupations requiring patience. This was different; he was reasonably safe inside the log house. It wasn't fear of being caught that bothered him, it was who might be his captor. If it was his nephew he did not doubt for one second what his fate would be. Kinship would not matter. The kind of blood-relationship between the old man and his nephew, or any of his nephew's friends, did not mean a thing.

He was not going to allow himself to be captured no matter who was out there.

He distinctly heard a shod horse move among tallis rock. Hair arose on the back of his neck. His horses were barefoot. The horses of his visitors had been freshly shod. But this sound had come from south of the house not north of it. He scrambled back onto the chair to look northward, and sure enough the horses which had been sunning themselves had not moved, had not stopped staring southward.

He climbed down, leaned against the door again, was about to abandon that when he heard a man say. 'Right here'll be good enough.' It was not possible through the door to identify the owner of the voice but he had a bad feeling the voice had belonged to his nephew.

The wounded man groaned. He was awake but to the old man his flushed face and dry eyes indicated he probably could not focus nor remember. Bligh said, 'Agnes, it warn't my fault.' Whatever else he said was indistinguishable.

Caulfield wiped off sweat. Remained by the door gazing at the wounded man, who seemed to be out of his head, even when he said, 'Water. Aggie I need some water.'

Caulfield knew about death and dying but he had never been comfortable with either, and in this respect he was no different from most other people, even calloused old mountain-dwelling frontiersmen.

He was about to get the bottle of whiskey when a very calm, quiet voice spoke behind him. 'Put the gun down. Put it atop the table.'

Caulfield turned slowly. A man he had never seen before was looking down at him from outside the high window.

'On the table!'

Caulfield obeyed.

The stranger had to be standing on something, maybe his saddle horse. Otherwise he would have had to be even taller than that beanpole from Cedarton.

They exchanged stares for several moments before the stranger spoke again. 'Un-bar the door an' open it – an' if you don't want to get bad hurt, stand where you can be seen from outside – with both hands in plain sight.'

Caulfield flicked a glance at the flush-faced man on the bunk. The stranger quietly said, 'The door, oldtimer.'

Caulfield lifted the *tranca*, opened the door and stood facing the very tall man with the blood-stiff sleeve with his partner the lawman from Cedarton. They were to one side of the old man's nephew and the renegade called Pat Ruggles, who was being supported by his captors. His head hung, his knees seemed sprung, he looked more dead than alive.

Ike addressed the old man. 'Who's in there with you?'

'The one called Bligh. He's the feller got shot near the edge of the arroyo.'

'Is he alive?'

'I think so, but he sure don't look good.'

Jered said, 'Walk backwards, Mister Caulfield. Keep in sight.'

They came to the doorway with the limp man between them. Only the old man's nephew was not cowed. He gave his uncle a cold look as he moved inside.

Not until the others were in the house did the stranger from the window appear. He was not as dirty, gaunt, sunken-eyed or as beard stubbled as the others. He was younger too, at least he appeared to be. Of them all his expression was totally blank.

They eased the limp man to the floor. Old Caulfield looked at him. His hair was matted with blood. The old man said, 'If he's shot in the head why'd you bother fetchin' him back here?'

Instead of replying Ike told the old man to get his whiskey if he had any. Caulfield dutifully retrieved the bottle from its hiding place.

Ike knelt, propped the outlaw against one leg and poured whiskey down him. The renegade flopped, coughed, gagged and flung his arms in all directions. Ike took him by the hair, bent his head back and poured in more whiskey about half of which spilled down the outlaw's shirtfront.

Ike then arose to hand back the bottle as he said, 'He'll be all right.'

Old Caulfield looked incredulous. 'Shot in the head, fer chriz'sake?'

Jered looked down. 'He got hit over the head, not shot.'

Caulfield turned to find the stranger standing like a stone looking toward the bunk. The old man explained where Bligh had been wounded. The stranger crossed to the bed, stood a moment gazing at the wounded man, drew his six-gun without haste and fired it. The sound inside the house was deafening. The stranger stood a moment looking at his victim then walked out of the house to care for his horse.

Bligh's right arm hung limply over the side of the bunk. The bullet had torn through his breastbone and heart. The old man was shocked into silence. When he tore his eyes away from the bed the very tall saloonman said, 'He's the one shot that feller's mother.' Jered did not explain how the stranger knew who had killed his mother on the porch of her home when she went outside to call her husband to breakfast, a call he hadn't heard because Porter Caulfield had crushed the old man's skull with a single tree.

No one ever explained that to the old man. To the day he died he tried to figure that out and never did.

Jered went to the water bucket, which was empty. He took it and left the house. Ike and the old man were alone except for the man on the floor beginning to feel warmed by the amount of whiskey which had been poured down him and Porter sitting near a pile of blankets.

Ike did not wait for the question. 'He tracked us. He's got a brother who stayed back to bury their folks. He was dry-camped at the southern end of the arroyo. Your nephew an' this feller run right onto him. He stopped your nephew from a distance of no more'n twenty feet. The feller on the floor was out front. The stranger caught him over the head before either of 'em knew anyone was in the dark down there.'

The old man asked a question just to be able to hear his own voice. Now he'd have to build a new bunk. 'What's his name?'

Ike was gazing at the corpse on the bunk when he replied. 'We didn't ask him. We come up when he was disarming your nephew. He didn't see us. We threw down on him ... We had no idea who he was. We talked a while then started back. This one on the floor slowed us considerable.' Ike jerked his head. 'Which one was the feller in the bunk?'

'Terry Bligh.' The old man nodded his head floorward, 'Which one of 'em is on the floor?'

'Pat Ruggles.'

'How hard did that feller hit him?'

Ike shrugged. 'Hard enough I guess. I got to go care for the horses.' As Ike said this he scooped up the six-gun atop the table and took it with him.

11

Four Horsemen

Daylight came all in a rush but the cold lingered and would continue to do so for another hour or two. The higher the altitude the longer it took for heat to come into each new day.

There was not much conversation as Ike and Jered went about caring for the animals. The stone-faced killer of Terry Bligh led his animal back far enough to find grass, and stopped dead still at sight of the corpse hanging from a tree limb, but only briefly, then continued on past until he could hobble his animal.

When he returned he leaned on a corral stringer, rolled and lighted a smoke and jerked his thumb backwards. 'Who's that?' he asked Jered. The very tall man answered in an equally terse voice.

'He was one of them. His name was John Bryan.'

The smoker considered Jered, then Ike, tipped ash and did not speak again until they were all inside where the old man agitatedly asked them to take that danged corpse off his bed.

They ignored him, got the man with the blood-matted hair to a chair and propped him there. He had the grandaddy of all headaches, otherwise he was conscious. He looked stonily at Porter Caulfield. 'Satisfied?' he snarled.

Caulfield did not answer. He was still sitting on the floor near the old man's pile of blankets. He watched the cowman more sharply than he watched the men from Cedarton. The cowman was deadly.

Jered told the old man to stoke his fire and rustle something to eat. Old Caulfield glared but obeyed. While he was at the stove he said, 'Take 'em out'n hang 'em. I don't have enough grub for all of you an' you're goin' to hang 'em anyway.'

The stranger went over by the stove to hold cold hands to the heat. The old man sidled away making it appear he did that in order to tend his fry pans better. The cowman gazed at him. He was not a visibly compassionate individual. The others had made that judgement before he shot Terry Bligh on the bed. Neither was he talkative.

Ike squatted near Porter Caulfield. 'You want to tell us you held the horses?'

Caulfield snarled, 'I tell you nothin'.'

Jered turned. 'Sure you will. You're goin' to sing like a bird.' Jered groped for his clasp-knife, opened it and regarded the sitting outlaw. 'It's dull,' he said, repeating what he had told the old man. 'So it don't cut, it sort of rips and tears.'

Caulfield snorted. 'You think I'm scairt?'

'You ought to be,' Jered replied.

The renegade showed scorn. 'What's goin' to happen directly will happen whether I talk or don't talk, an' right now I don't figure to tell you a damned thing.'

The man on the chair addressed Ike, ignoring Caulfield. 'What d'you want to know?'

'Where the band of you come from, how you happened to raid in Cedar Valley?'

The man with the headache had enough whiskey in him to cooperate; enough for him to be sly as well. 'We come up from down south.'

'Raided your way?'

'Yes. Sometimes we hit 'em about sunup. Dependin' on whether they had hired riders. If they did have, we'd wait out of sight until the riders left the yard.'

Ike thought the outlaw was probably telling the truth so he asked him about the raid on the Garfield place. Ruggles ignored the cold, murderous look he was getting from Porter Caulfield. 'We scouted up the place. There was sign of hired riders but we didn't see 'em. Port said they had gone south with a drive, most likely. He knew the folks.

'We come in fast, was out front before the women knew who we was. One of 'em tall as a man, run back inside. The other two … we talked to …'

'And shot?' Ike asked.

'Well, they had guns in the house.'

The cowman turned from warming his hands. 'They was on the porch?'

'Yes.'

'Then how did you know they had guns in the house?'

Ruggles cleared his throat, refused to look at the cowman and spoke instead to Ike Bowen. 'They always got guns in the house.'

The cowman stood a moment regarding the outlaw. Ike thought he knew what was coming, got between them with his back to the cowman and said. 'What about the girl in the hay mow?'

Ruggles very gently wagged his head. 'I don't know how she got around us to get up there. Maybe while we was ransackin' the house. Anyway, when we come for the horses, she commenced firing. We fired back, drove her deeper into the mow, got astride and was runnin' out of the yard when she commenced shootin' again. This time we kept on going. I think she emptied her guns because we was still in sight when the firin' stopped.'

Old Caulfield put food in tin dishes and put them on the table. He did not set a place for himself. Every time he looked sideways he saw that limp hand and arm over the side of his bunk.

They fed Ruggles but Porter Caulfield did not approach the table so they ignored him.

The old man made chicory coffee black as original sin and powerful enough to shrivel the *pelotes* on a brass monkey. It had an unusually bitter taste because as the coffee got low in its jar the old man would boil a few juniper berries and mix them with the coffee beans.

No one minded. The old man couldn't have cooked for a band of Digger Indians, but that did not much matter either. They ate in silence, drank the coffee, arose and went outside, all but the old man, who gazed bleakly at his nephew as he said, 'Sure as hell they'll hang you like they done that feller up in the trees, an' I'm goin' to tell you I want to watch 'em do it.'

Caulfield turned on his uncle. 'You got a boot knife; give it to me.'

The old man smiled. 'Where's yours, you always carried one. Did they find it?'

'No. Give me your knife for Pat.'

The old man looked over at the man on the chair and slowly wagged his head. 'He can't handle no knife, Porter. Not in his shape.'

'Give me your damned knife, you old screwt!'

The old man smiled again. 'Use your own. Damned idiot, there's three of 'em all armed to the teeth. You try usin' a knife an' they'll salt you down with lead … One time I told your mother you had guts, but didn't have a lick of common sense.'

The younger man glared, 'I should have shot you. We didn't need you, only your shack.'

The old man's eyes were fierce. 'That's what I meant to your maw. You don't have the sense gawd give a goose. All your life there was things you'd ought to have done an' lacked the sense to do 'em.'

Porter Caulfield turned toward the injured outlaw. 'You got a knife, Pat?'

'Yes.'

'Get ready to use it when they come back inside.'

Ruggles made no move to lean, lift his trouser leg for the boot-knife, he sat gazing at the other renegade until Port said, 'Pat, they're goin' to hang us. Anything's better'n just settin' here until they come back. There's a chance we can cut our way clear, settin' here we got no chance at all.'

Ruggles still did not move. The old man turned, casually re-filled a dented tin cup with his back to the stove sipping. He was enjoying this right up until a faint breeze wafted gut-shot bear-scent inside the house. He put the cup aside and emptied coffee grounds into the firebox of the stove and removed all iron lids. Burning coffee grounds helped but not entirely.

His nephew watched the old man. 'You got shells for that old shotgun?' he asked.

The old man answered facing the stove. 'No. Only the two in the chambers.'

Port's eyes brightened. 'That's all I need.' He leaned to arise from the floor at the same moment the men from Cedarton and the cowman walked in out of the rotting-bear-scented sunshine. Jered told Porter to sit back down. The old man cackled. 'He was fixin' to get that old shotgun.'

Ike's eyes widened. 'Is it loaded?'

'What the hell good is an unloaded gun? Of course it's loaded.'

Jered crossed over, picked up the gun, snapped it open, removed the pair of cartridges, tossed the gun aside and asked the old man if there were other loaded weapons in the cabin.

Old Caulfield snarled his answer. 'For lawmen you sure is careless. That's the only other gun beside the pistol I had. There's a Sharp's army carbine under the bed but I never been able to find loads for it. Bought if off a soldier about the time you was born.'

Jered knelt to look beneath the bunk. There was

drying blood under there. He saw the old army weapon and left it where it was. As he arose he looked at Ike and the cowman. 'You ready? No sense in draggin' this out.'

They were ready. Jered told the pair of renegades to stand up. Caulfield came up to his feet with no effort but the man with the matted hair was slower. He had to steady himself with a hand on the back of the chair. The armed men watched. Each one made a mistaken judgment; Pat Ruggles was not unsteady because of his lost blood or his injury, he was about half drunk.

The old man rubbed calloused palms together. He anticipated the lynching with relish. Jered asked if Ruggles needed someone to lean on. The outlaw glared. 'Not from the likes of you, beanpole.'

Jered was unaffected. 'It's a fair hike from here to them trees.'

Ruggles glared without speaking.

They herded the renegades outside where the sun was high, dozens of blue-tailed flies were hovering around the bear carcass, and the loose-stock was beginning to drift away now that they were warm. They went in the direction of the rocked-spring.

Ruggles was inclined to yaw a little as he was driven around the corral. No one offered to help him this time. Porter Caulfield walked steadily northward in the direction of his former companion still hanging from a tree limb. His face was stone-set, his jaws were locked hard. He was still defiant. He was also exasperated that he hadn't had a chance to escape because, as he had told Ruggles, they were going to hang anyway, so they might as well resist for all they were worth. It was better to die fighting than to die passively like sheep.

The sun was near its meridian, heat was noticeable even among the trees. Something else was noticeable: Rotting bear scent. In fact buzzards were circling in high, ragged circles.

The old man who had trooped along in the wake of the others, looked up with his lips working. He was about as fond of buzzards as he was of blue jays.

It required time to locate two more thick, low limbs. When they found them Jered went back for rope. There was no great hurry now. Caulfield faced Ike and the cowman. 'I don't suppose you fellers ever did anythin' bad.'

The cold-eyed cowman gazed at Caulfield without making a sound. He would have killed him in cold blood if he could. Back at the cabin he could have, but having gone along with the others it was now too late.

Ike groped for a cigar, found it had been broken, plugged one half between his teeth, regarded Pat Ruggles, who was pale and sweaty. Ike said, 'Set down before you fall down.'

Ruggles sank to the ground. His headache had diminished a little but not much. He was drunk and knew it. His thoughts came and went, he made no attempt to control them, to concentrate. Ironically, in his present frame of mind he was grateful for shade.

Caulfield sneered. 'You fellers lived lily-white lives.' He snorted. 'You're hypocrites, that's what you are.'

Ike finally put his attention upon the renegade. 'It goes without sayin' that a man don't reach my age without doin' a few things he ain't proud of. But not murder, Caulfield. Not killin' an old man with a single tree, not deliberately shootin' women.'

The outlaw continued to sneer. He did not look at the cowman standing there like a big stone gazing with total distraction at Caulfield. There was not an inch of the cowman that could be appealed to. He addressed Ike again. 'We got enough cached away to make you gents independent for life. You could go anywhere you liked and live like kings.'

The cowman's gaze did not waver. He might as well have been deaf. Ike's attention was distracted by the old man who chirped his two-bits' worth. 'Port, you danged fool, whatever you got squirreled away … It's way too late. That's somethin' else I'll tell your maw when next I see her. You just ain't very smart.'

Caulfield snarled at his uncle, 'Shut up, you old fool. If it wasn't for you I wouldn't be standin' here now. You tell my maw how you turned traitor against your own kin. She'll take a horsewhip to you.'

The rugged rancher tired of this and finally spoke. He had Porter Caulfield skewered with an unblinking stare. 'Mister, if we was alone I know ways to kill you so slow it'd take two days for you to die.'

Caulfield finally looked at the cowman. His expression of contempt faded. He had up to now never faltered with vituperation. He and the cowman looked steadily at each other for several moments before Caulfield turned away from the man who had stood gazing at Caulfield's partner in the bunk, and had without haste drawn his sidearm and had shot Terry Bligh as calmly and as coldly as a man might shoot a rattlesnake.

Jered returned with ropes. He moved past the cowman to a thick low limb, pitched the rope over it and was fashioning a slip-knot when Pat Ruggles fell over without a sound. Ike looked down as Jered said, 'Fainted. Now we got to wait.'

The cowman shook his head. 'Hang the son of a bitch. Get this over with.'

Ike knelt to remove the unconscious man's belt and grope for his bandana. He secured the man's ankles with the belt, rolled him over to tie both arms in back using the bandana then hoisted Ruggles into a sitting posture with his back to the hang-tree.

Jered knelt to slip the rope around Ruggles's neck as he said, 'He's goin' to be one surprised son of a bitch when he comes around.'

The cowman moved in to help Jered lift the unconscious man. He would have preferred waiting for Ruggles to regain consciousness before hanging him, but Jered was hoisting the renegade to his feet so the cowman helped steady him while Ike took the required dallies around the tree. Ike was ready to nod for them to lift when the old man made a squawking sound. He was staring round-eyed beyond them up through the timber. Ike, Jered and the cowman paused to look in the same direction.

Three men were balancing carbines across saddle seats. A fourth man was sitting his horse, leaning on the saddlehorn. He had a harsh voice when he said, 'Untie him!'

The startled lynchers stood stone still until one of the men aiming across the seat of his saddle cocked his Winchester. The mounted man spoke again.

'*Untie him!*'

Jered eased the unconscious man down. Ruggles collapsed in a heap. The horseman gave another order. 'Now the other one.'

Jered started to protest. The other two men cocked their carbines; Jered's protest died aborning. Ike dropped the dallied rope and went to help Jered free Caulfield.

The cowman said, 'They're murderers an' worse. Set them free, you don't know what you're doing.'

The mounted man considered the speaker for a long moment. 'Ain't you one of old man Hamilton's boys?'

The cowman nodded. 'I'm Pete, the oldest one. My brother's back at the yard buryin' my folks. These murdering bastards killed them both ... They're renegades.'

The mounted man looped his reins, raised a plug and bit off a corner, cheeked it without taking his eyes off the cowman. He dismounted, trailed one rein in his left hand and said, 'I'm Alfred Morgan. We found two of my best horses down south with saddles on 'em. Tell me somethin', Mister Hamilton, how come a self-respectin' stockman to be ridin' with horsethieves?'

Jered, Ike and the cowman stared. Ike spoke first. 'My name's Bowen, I'm the constable down at Cedarton. Me'n Mister Salte here, been trackin' these renegades since they murdered Neil Garfield's wife an' one of his daughters ... They raided this cowman's place, killed his maw an' paw. We trailed them up here,' Ike jerked his head sideways 'to this place. It belongs to the old man yonder. His name is Caulfield, an' that's his nephew. His name is Porter Caulfield ... There's another one in the house. He's dead. That one hangin' in the tree was one of them. There's another back some miles. We caught him in his bedroll. He's dead too.'

Alfred Morgan stood listening until Ike finished, then he said, 'What we want to know, mister, is who stole my two horses?'

Jered, more than a head taller than the others, looked down his nose at Alfred Morgan. 'Me'n the constable took them. Our horses was wore out we was gettin' close to the renegades – so we took the first horses we come to. Otherwise we couldn't have got up here while it was too dark for them to see us coming. That's pretty much open country back yonder.'

Alfred Morgan was not a tall man but was thick and powerful. His eyes were habitually narrowed from a lifetime out of doors. His skin was permanently tanned. He had a slightly hooked nose and a jaw as square as granite.

He shifted his narrowed eyes from one of them

to the other without speaking, which gave Porter Caulfield the opportunity he needed. Porter was quick-witted; he had recovered from the surprise before the others. He had also sized-up Alfred Morgan. Now he spoke into the silence. 'Mister, they're lyin' through their teeth. Them two, the beanpole an' his friend, come ridin' up here lookin' for a place to hide out after stealin' two horses. The rest of what that one just told you was made up out of pure lies.'

Morgan put his attention on the craggy cowman. 'Mister Hamilton – why was you ridin' with horsethieves?'

Hamilton gave a delayed reply. 'I come after the fellers who killed my folks. These other two were already up here. I helped 'em catch one on the ground an' Caulfield. That's all I can tell you. I never seen the horses they rode up here on.'

Porter Caulfield had driven his wedge. He scowled at Alfred Morgan. 'Does that satisfy you? I'll tell you the rest of it: Them two from Cedarton was goin' to lynch us for our outfits. They're renegades, Mister Morgan. Pure an' simple – they're murderin', horse-stealin', renegades!'

12

One Left

Morgan faced his three riders, hard, tough rangemen. 'Well now, what d'you boys think?'

One man said, 'Someone's got to be lyin', Al.'

Another rider, clearly more like his employer, in that he thought only about their stolen horses, made his judgement in a few words. 'Hang the lot of 'em.'

Pete Hamilton broke his silence. 'Mister Morgan, you knew my folks.'

'For a fact I did. We been neighbours for twenty years.'

The taciturn man's reply to that was simple. 'You know damned well I'm no horsethief.'

'I didn't figure to hang you too.'

'Then you better believe that one on the ground an' his partner have been murderin' folks – other than my maw and paw.'

Morgan accepted that. 'All right. We'll hang 'em.'

That Morgan rider who evidently thought about one thing at a time and would not be influenced, repeated his earlier remark. 'We got two horsethieves an' what looks like maybe two renegades. Let's hang all of 'em.'

Jered addressed this rangeman. 'We told you how we happened to take your horses, mister. You'd have done the same if you'd been in our boots.'

The rangeman shook his head at Jered. 'Mister, I wouldn't have stole a horse, no matter what.'

Ike pegged this Morgan-rider for what he was; an individual who knew only right and wrong, black and white, with no extenuating circumstance. He faced the rancher, brought forth the badge from his pocket and held it on his palm.

The dogmatic rider snorted. 'I've seen them things pass back an' forth in poker games.'

Caulfield spoke up. 'He showed us that badge too. That's how him an' his long-legged friend got our confidence. Mister Morgan …'

Old man Caulfield interrupted. 'You always was a liar,' he told his nephew. 'Since you was a little kid you lied when the truth would have fit better.'

Morgan faintly frowned at the old man. 'If you're his uncle, why did they come to you – if they're really renegades?'

The old man was fidgeting again. 'Why? Because he's done it before; figured me being blood-kin he could come up here with his killers an' I'd let 'em lie over until they was ready to go back to murderin' folks.'

That dogmatic rangeman said, 'You own guns, do you mister?'

The old man flared up. 'What kind of silly

damned fool question is that? Cowboy, you know folks who live this far from anywhere that don't have guns? Of course I got guns.'

'Then when you seen them comin' why didn't you throw down on them?'

That was too much for Jered. He glared at the Morgan-rider. 'One old man against ... Mister, his pistol's one of them oldtime hawglegs with a barrel a foot long. He's got a shotgun made before I was born, an' an old army carbine you can't buy bullets for any more. But if he'd had a Gatling gun you think one old man could run off four renegades?'

Morgan said, 'Four?'

Jered turned on him too. 'Ike told you – we caught one in his camp miles back. We socked him away. That left four.'

The first of the Morgan-riders to speak, a man who was more thoughtful than the dogmatic rider, spoke again. 'You and the lawman hung that feller over yonder?'

Jered nodded.

'How'd you separate him from his friends?'

'They holed-up in the cabin. That one, his name was Bryan, come outside to pee. Ike grabbed him.'

When Jered stopped speaking Porter Caulfield made a derisive snort. 'That part's the truth, gent. Me'n my friends was restin' in the cabin with no reason to figure outlaws was sneakin' around outside. Not until we seen Bryan hangin' from that tree did we figure they was around. Horse-stealin' outlaws!'

The other Morgan-rider eased back, grounded his Winchester and shook his head without speaking. Ike turned to the old man. 'Tell 'em,' he ordered.

The old man obeyed. Addressing the rancher he began at the beginning. Several times Porter Caulfield would have interrupted but Al Morgan levelled a finger and said, 'Not a damned word.'

The old man finished, nudged Jered who understood the purpose of the nudge and handed the old man his plug. Alfred Morgan tied his horse to a low limb, raised his hat, scratched and lowered the hat. His riders, still with Winchesters, regarded their employer. That dogmatic one adhered to his conviction, he favoured hanging them all.

The other two riders were hesitant, as was Morgan. He asked Ike if the old man had told the truth. Ike replied that he could not vouch for what the old man had said about things at the clearing before he and Jered had got up there, but everything the old man had said afterwards was the gospel truth.

The dogmatic rider asked about the bear. Ike started to explain and was interrupted by the old man's nephew.

'They shot him in the dark. Me'n my friends was inside the shack. That's when we knew we had enemies up here.'

The old man snorted. 'Damned liar; they was outside when the bear pulled the chain loose and went lookin' for someone to kill. They run into the house – all but one man; he shot the bear, then he got into the house. Mister, they forted-up. I already told you the rest of it.'

Al Morgan leaned against a tree. After a long

silence he jerked his head for the taciturn cowman named Pete Hamilton to walk back through the trees with him. The others watched.

Pat Ruggles moaned and raised a hand to his blood-matted hair. Porter Caulfield hissed at him, 'Not a word, Pat. Don't you open your mouth.'

That thoughtful tall rangeman regarded Caulfield. 'He'll talk, mister. Believe me he'll talk … What is it you don't want him to say?'

Ike was interested in Caulfield's reply. Ruggles had spoken frankly inside the cabin. The old man's nephew was regarding the slumped man with the matted hair when he replied to the Morgan-rider. 'His name's Pat. He ain't bright. I've known him for years. I know for a fact he'll tell you what he figures you want to know.'

'What's wrong with that?' the rangeman asked. 'What we want to know is – who's a liar here an' who ain't.'

Caulfield looked pityingly at Pat Ruggles. 'He ain't quite right in the head, mister. He's like one of them parrots, whatever he hears he repeats. You say to him that he killed folks an' he'll repeat it back for you.'

The rangeman soberly regarded Pat Ruggles, he looked a little pityingly as he said, 'Partner, d'you know this Caulfield feller?'

Pat looked up at the old man's nephew. 'Yep, I know him. I've rode with him some years now. His name's –'

'How many folks has he killed?' the rangeman asked.

Pat's eyes came back slowly to the stockman.

'Him? He never killed no one.' Pat pointed toward Ike. 'That one has. Him'n his friend has.'

The Morgan-riders looked steadily at Ike Bowen. For his part, Ike had been impressed by Pat Ruggles' ability to act the part of a dim-wit. He really was not altogether bright, but for a fact he was sly. Ike gazed at the seated man and gently shook his head.

The riders clubbed together to whisper. As they did this Porter Caulfield leaned down to scratch his leg. Everything he desperately needed was tantalisingly close at hand; a horse, weapons, a decent chance to acquire both and run for it.

But the odds were formidable. Caulfield forgot about the only remaining member of his marauder band. They could do with Pat whatever they chose to do.

The old man sat down. He seemed to have aged ten years in the past day or two, but he was still caustic. As a matter of fact he would remain that way until folks patted him in the face with a shovel a few years later.

Caulfield was scheming when the rancher and Pete Hamilton returned from among the trees walking side by side. Neither man showed any expression.

Hamilton went over beside Ike and stood like a tree as Morgan jerked his head for Port Caulfield to also go among the trees with him. Morgan palmed his six-gun as he walked behind Caulfield. Ike made a quiet observation: 'He better keep distance between 'em.'

One of the Morgan-riders spoke just as quietly. 'He didn't come down in the last rain, mister.'

Heat increased the decomposing of the bear. The longer he would lie there the more he smelled to high heaven. Even the old man looked pained and he was probably accustomed to such odours.

The discussion between Alfred Morgan and Porter Caulfield took half the time the rancher's earlier conversation with Pete Hamilton had taken. When they returned from the timber Caulfield strolled over near his uncle, who turned his back on him as Morgan huddled briefly with his riders. Ike and Jered watched the huddle. They had both been impressed with Porter Caulfield's ability to lie and make his lies sound believable.

When the stockmen broke up their palaver Alfred Morgan nodded in Caulfield's direction. The two of them left the trees in the direction of the cabin. The smell down there was almost overpowering and those circling high buzzards were now making their sweeps much lower; if the two-legged creatures hadn't been in sight, they would have flocked over the carcass.

Morgan was, as his rider had dryly said, no novice. He had Caulfield on the left side. Morgan's holstered Colt was on the right side.

They entered the cabin with the watchers among the trees neither moving nor speaking. Morgan's hired hands seemed to Constable Bowen to be anticipating something. Ike was totally in the dark but he assumed there was going to be some kind of decision soon.

Jered looked at Pat Ruggles. He had slumped against the tree and was asleep. Jered shook his head. Ruggles had not impressed the saloonman as being half an imbecile, but right now Jered was less sure. No one teetering between being hanged and not being hanged, would go to sleep.

One of the Morgan-riders un-looped a battered old canteen and drank from it. He offered the canteen to his companions, they shook their heads. The old man held out his hand. The cowboy considered the hand, the old man, stoppered his canteen and re-draped it from the saddlehorn. The old man flared up. 'Let me tell you, even In'ians never refused water to a man. Not even when they had a prisoner.'

He got no reply, the riders were again watching the cabin.

Morgan and Caulfield emerged. Ike tried to anticipate what would now ensue from their faces. He might as well have been studying rocks.

Caulfield veered off to go over where he had been sitting near his uncle. The old man acted as though his nephew did not exist.

Across from them, with Ike and Jered watching, the riders and their employer palavered again, keeping their voices low.

The buzzards were now making clumsy runs on the ground, anxious to feast and willing to incur risks. They did not really fear men very much; everyone in cattle country realised buzzards were necessary scavengers despite their sickening odour and ugliness. The few people who had ever gotten close to buzzards knew something else; the big birds could not get airborne without running along the ground, then springing into the air. Those who overtook buzzards never repeated the process; the bird's defence in a close encounter was to vomit. Because they were carrion eaters, such encounters were not only disgusting but no amount of scrubbing ever got the smell out of the cloth.

They also fought and screamed at one another, which they did now as the men up in the timber ignored them when Alfred Morgan moved clear of his riders looking straight at Ike Bowen.

Before speaking he brought forth a handful of jewelry, gold coins and several pocket watches, also of gold. He was looking straight at the constable when he said, 'Tie 'em, lads.'

His riders left their carbines with the horses and started forward, got in front and behind Porter Caulfield and went to work. The renegade struggled and cursed. They had to throw him on the ground but they got his arms secured behind his back and lashed his ankles before they yanked him back upright. Caulfield yelled at Morgan. 'You double-crossin' son of a bitch.'

Morgan smiled. 'Nobody but a damned fool would expect me to accept your offer of this loot to let you go – when by handin' me these things from the cache under the straw mattress where that dead man was lyin' proved who the renegades was an' who they wasn't.'

Ike heard Jered's breath come out slowly. The old man was on his feet. 'I told you, dang it. I told you exactly how it all happened. Trouble with folks like you, Mister Morgan, you wouldn't know the truth if a man was standin' on ten feet of Bibles when he said it.'

They ignored old Caulfield. Ruggles slept

through everything, his body slumped half against a rough-barked tree, slightly folded forward. Jered softly wagged his head. Ruggles could probably sleep through the end of the world.

Caulfield never stopped fighting. He called Morgan and his riders every name he could think of. He particularly cursed the rancher for accepting Caulfield's offer for his loot in exchange for freedom, then betraying him for being the only man who knew where that loot had been cached, the only man who had taken it from his victims.

Even with three strong rangeriders restraining him the renegade fought, struggled, swore and roared. When he fell a Morgan-rider leaned and picked up the boot-knife. They had not found the knife during their struggle and Caulfield had not had an opportunity to use it. That tall, thoughtful rangeman retrieved the knife, stood in front of Caulfield with the blade pointing, and shook his head, flung the knife away as Al Morgan told them to carry Caulfield if they had to, but take him up where that rope was still dallied around the tree.

They actually did have to carry him. He threw himself down rolled and tried to bunch his bound ankles to kick, he cursed and yelled. Jered and Ike went over to assist. They and the three Morgan riders lifted Caulfield, carried him to the hang-tree and dropped him.

Ike and Jered returned to the place where they had been standing as Al Morgan walked over, offered his hand to taciturn Pete Hamilton, then with equal gravity shook hands with both Ike and Jered.

He turned and told his riders to gag Caulfield, whose yelling was getting on the rancher's nerves.

Another struggle followed. Caulfield bit a hand, twisted his head, spat, locked his jaw. He was sweating hard, he was red in the face.

Ike watched the dogmatic rangeman pick up a stick, shove it forcefully into the side of Caulfield's mouth and pry the renegade's jaws apart. Another rangeman shoved a bandana into place. When the stick was withdrawn the man with both ends of the gag tied them tightly and stood up nursing a bitten finger. As he drew back a foot his employer growled at him.

The old man had stood apart during the fight. He remained clear of the struggle but when they had Porter on his feet, a man holding him from each side, the old man walked close and said, 'You like to got me killed, you ruined my cabin, you never been up here you ain't caused me misery … I ain't goin' to tell your maw a danged thing. When these gents is through I'm goin' to bury you in the same hole as that stinkin' bear.' The old man was turning away when he said, 'Good riddance.'

Ike and Jered felt the bound man straining against his bindings. He was not only defiant, he was wildly so.

Al Morgan came over, looked Caulfield in the eyes and said, 'My maw taught me the worst people was entitled to a prayer for their rotten souls. Caulfield, maybe someone else'll do that for you, I won't.'

He stepped back, waited until Ike had snugged his hitches then nodded his head for the men holding Caulfield to lift him. This time there were enough men to hoist him more than two feet in the air. Caulfield's eyes bulged, a vein in the side of his neck swelled. He made strangling noises behind his gag.

Morgan looked him straight in the eyes as he nodded his head for the holders to release him.

Even the old man was awed by the wild threshing as his nephew fought for his life. That thoughtful rangeman turned away, no one else did.

As the struggles became weaker, though, all but the old man turned away. He seemed to enjoy the final death struggles of his nephew.

The buzzards were squawking, screeching at one another, fighting, dragging bear parts in all directions. The sun was high, the air was still, there was heat in the day.

Ike turned once. Now there were two men hanging lifeless among the trees. He started toward the cabin, Jered called and led the way to the rocked-up spring instead.

13

The Ride Back

When Ike and Jered returned from the spring old man Caulfield and the others were standing around the remaining renegade. It only dawned on the two men from Cedarton at the last moment that Pat Ruggles hadn't fallen asleep. He was dead.

Morgan soberly said, 'It saves us a hangin'.'

That dogmatic rider of his was neither awed by death nor compassionate in the face of it. 'I was lookin' forward to yankin' him up.'

Several men looked at him but said nothing. Even the old man was silent, possibly because the slumped man by the tree did not look dead, he looked asleep.

Al Morgan turned his back on the dead man. 'Mister Caulfield, you got a lot of diggin' to do. Them dead men an' that bear.'

Caulfield jerked straight up. 'Me? I didn't kill none of 'em, not even the bear. Why should I have to –'

'Because this here is your property,' stated

Morgan, using a variety of logic that seemed to appear proper to Morgan and his riders.

The old man had a fit. 'None of this was my affair. Hell, I only lived up here mindin' my own business. I didn't know they was comin', never wanted 'em here.' He cleared his throat. 'I had nothin' to do with any of it. Least you fellers could do is help me dig the graves.'

Morgan was expressionless when he replied. 'We got work to do, Mister Caulfield. We had to interrupt some markin' an' brandin', an' it's waiting for us.'

One of Morgan's riders went after their horses, when he returned the other horses followed including the animals Ike and Jered had 'borrowed.'

That dogmatic cowboy watched the horses being corralled and growled, 'A man who steals a horse is a horsethief no matter what.'

Jered approached the cowboy. He towered over him. 'Borrowed,' he said quietly. 'You already know why.'

Before trouble could erupt Al Morgan told his rider to go help with the horses. As soon as the man was gone Morgan looked at Ike. 'You ride back with us. We'll bring in your animals an' you boys can be on your way.'

Ike's response only pleased one man. He said, 'That'll be one hell of a chore diggin' all those graves, Mister Morgan. Jered an' I'll stay back an' help the old man.'

Morgan's dilemma was simple; if he trailed his horses away with him the two men from Cedarton would be afoot. He looked at his riders and sighed. 'Let's get started on the diggin', it's goin' to be hot directly.'

Old Caulfield smiled broadly at Ike, but when they approached the cabin they encountered a serious problem. The old man only owned two pick-axes and two shovels.

Jered volunteered to man one pick and one shovel, but Morgan assigned one of his riders to use the pick-axe while Jered manned a shovel.

Morgan assigned another rider to Isaac Bowen to also work as a team. His remaining rider, the tall, thoughtful man did not act particularly relieved when Morgan said, 'You'n Will get a rope on each front paw of the bear, drag him to the edge of the arroyo and roll him over.'

The tall man looked sceptical. 'Al, there ain't a horse up here that'll stand bein' within a hunnert feet of that stinkin' bear.'

Another Morgan-rider made a suggestion no one even considered. 'Me'n my paw killed a bear near the house one time. Big 'un. We piled dry wood over the carcass an' burnt it down to ash.'

Only one man responded. Old Caulfield reacted as though he'd been bee-stung. 'You danged idiot; the whole country's dryer'n tinder!'

The cowboy's suggestion died right there. The old man's indignation was justified and they all knew it – all but the dogmatic rangeman whose suggestion it had been.

While the others leaned on shovels watching, Morgan and his rider went to the corral, rigged out their animals, shook down their lass ropes and rode around the corral toward the bear carcass and the small crowd of watchers.

They did not even get close. The smell alone was overpowering, but it was *bear* smell. Morgan was fudging his terrified horse around the bear when the mount of his companion took to him for all he was worth. The quiet man rode him out right up until he sunfished, sprang high into the air and swapped ends. Very few men could ride out something like that even in a bronc saddle.

The quiet man lost his hat, then one stirrup, and finally sailed from the saddle like a bird. He landed so hard Jered had to help him up. He sucked air and blinked while the terrified horse stuck his tail in the air and ran.

With a curse Al Morgan went after him, still with his lass rope in his right hand.

The last any of them saw was when the panicked horse, head high to avoid stepping on the reins, stirrups flopping, headed for one of those game trails down into the arroyo.

Ike calmly said, 'Now we're goin' to be shy a mount.'

Of the two remaining Morgan-riders, one of them said, 'He'll catch him.'

Jered looked at the old man. 'How about your sorrels?'

Caulfield fairly spat his response. 'You seen what happened, didn't you? If you wasn't a town person you'd know better'n to even ask ... That was a damnfool thing to try. Ain't a horse alive that'll get near that stinkin' bear.'

Jered was using his hat to beat dust off the dazed

rangeman when the old man suddenly said, 'Simon! What'n hell you doin' on my land?'

A man as old as Caulfield was sitting just north of the corral atop a big Missouri mule. He ignored old Caulfield, his interest was on the others and the dead bear.

He was attired in buckskin, except for an old army forage cap from which the stars and bars emblem had been removed. He spat amber, climbed down holding a long-barrelled old rifle. He had a two-foot fleshing knife on one side of his belt and another of those old, long-barrelled hawgleg pistols on the other side. He spat again then replied to Caulfield.

'I heard shootin', figured with any luck someone had killed you, but my luck ain't been good lately.'

Caulfield snarled back, 'I told you the last time I caught you settin' wolf traps on my land, to get away an' stay away.'

The other old man, who had a trimmed beard and small dark eyes, put his gaze upon old Caulfield. 'Jake, you never had the brains gawd give a chicken. Why'd you shoot a bear in hot weather in front of your house?'

'I didn't shoot the son of a bitch, an' I meant it about you stayin' a mile off on your own land. Every blessed word of it!'

The old mountaineer continued to regard Caulfield calmly. 'Well, you gents goin' to stand around until that bear-stink drives you out of the country?'

No one mentioned what had happened. Jered addressed the mule-man. 'You got some ideas how to get rid of the bear, mister?'

The little dark eyes came to rest on tall Jered. The

old man did as most folks did, he began at Jered's boots and went up to the crown of his hat. He asked the particular question that irritated the saloonman. 'How tall are you, friend?'

Jered had a spiteful answer ready when Ike elbowed him. Jered replied matter-of-factly. 'Six foot an' seven inches. Any other personal questions you want to ask, Mister …?'

'Cap'n Kirk, tall man. Cap'n Kirk, Army of Northern Virginia.'

Caulfield snarled again. 'Damned rebel. He's been a bother to me since I found him settin' traps on my land seven years back.'

Jered ignored the old man's outburst, he was accustomed to them by now. 'Captain, what can you do with that big mule?'

The old man leaned on his rifle considering the men looking at him. 'I expect you're thinkin' can my mule drag that carcass away.'

'Can he?' Jered asked.

'He can, only I got no right to be on Jake Caulfield's land. You heard the old screwt.' The old man turned to mount the large mule.

The Morgan-rider who had been jumped off had completely recovered. He spoke quietly to the old Rebel. 'We'd take it kindly, Captain, if you'd see if you can get your mule close enough for us to put ropes on the bear.'

The old man turned. 'I told you, I ain't welcome here.'

Caulfield was about to agree with that when Ike reached, held the old man's arm and squeezed, kept squeezing. Caulfield danced like a monkey on a string. He even tried to hit Ike. Bowen caught the flailing arm and forced it down. 'You want to live with that stinkin' bear in front of your house until winter?' Ike swung the old man to face his adversary beside his placid big mule. 'Ask him to help with the bear.'

'I wouldn't ask that danged old Rebel for water if I was dyin' of thirst,' Caulfield exclaimed.

Ike bent the old man's arm up between his shoulders in back, paused when the old man squeaked. 'Ask him or I'll break your arm.' Ike increased pushing until Caulfield would have bent forward if he could have. The pain was excruciating. He gasped between clenched jaws, 'Simon … help 'em with the bear.'

Ike pushed. Caulfield bleated. 'Simon … Please help 'em get rid of the bear.'

Ike released the old man as the mountaineer spat again, talked to his mule and started around the corral as he said, 'Couple of you boys put ropes on his front end.'

Not a word was spoken as the old Rebel and his mule walked around in front of the carcass where two of Morgan's riders had made ropes fast around each huge paw, breathing through their mouths as they did so, then went over where the others were standing in front of the cabin.

The mule showed absolutely no hint of panic as he waited for his owner to take dallies on the saddlehorn. Jered leaned toward Ike Bowen. 'I never saw the like.' A rangeman standing nearby said, 'An' I'd bet money you never will see the like again. I've owned my share of mules; they ain't as spooky as horses, but they're just as scairt of bears as horses are. If that mule don't run away when the old man moves him I'll eat my hat.'

They heard someone coming down in the arroyo, but their interest was on the old man and his big mule. He went around front, talked to the mule and eased him forward by the cheek-piece until all the slack had been taken up. He then talked to him again and the mule leaned into the rearward weight.

At first the carcass did not move. The mule leaned more, until he had the carcass moving before he raised a front hoof. He dragged the bear leaving behind black blood, hundreds of agitated flies who danced around the corpse as it was dragged away.

Jered removed the hat of the rangeman near him, handed it to the man and said, 'Eat.'

There were chuckles but no loud laughter. They were watching the corpse being dragged away. Once, when the old Rebel stopped, Jake Caulfield yelled to him. 'Keep goin', Simon.'

The old mule-man called back. 'You know how to say please, Jake?'

'Please, gawdamn your Confederate soul!'

The mule started forward. The ground sloped slightly southward, which helped, but the old man's big Missouri critter had twice the strength of most horses, as a saddle animal he was like riding a small continuing series of earthquakes, but for collar-strength, or, in this instance, saddlehorn strength he could out-pull just about anything with four legs and ears.

The mule stopped suddenly as a rider emerged from the arroyo leading a sweat-shiny saddled horse. Alfred Morgan also halted. The old Rebel said, 'Just stay where you are, mister, I'll sashay around an' keep goin',' which he did but even then Morgan's horses were on the edge of panic until the mule and his bear were farther southward, then Morgan took his animals back up where men were watching, open-mouthed.

As he handed the reins to the quiet man who had been bucked off he said, 'I thought you'd have at least a couple of graves dug by now.'

The digging teams went to work. Old Caulfield only stopped squinting southward when Morgan told him to fetch drinking water from the spring.

They eventually had to abandon digging to throw dirt over the caked blood; flies were all over the place, bothering the diggers, even flying into the cabin where it was not very light.

Caulfield was inside cooking food when his neighbour walked in without making a sound until he leaned his rifle aside. Before Caulfield could speak the other old man said, 'I left him quite a ways south. Them danged buzzards was almost as tame as chickens ... What's you cookin'?'

'Muskrat, wild onions and rutabagas. You hungry, Simon?'

'Danged seldom ain't, Jake.' The old Rebel wrinkled his nose. 'Smells good ... I got thinking when I was draggin' that bear away – what the hell was all the shootin' about, an' there's some fellers hangin' in trees up yonder.'

Without looking up from the stove Caulfield

said, 'There's another one on the bed.'

The mountaineer turned and stared. 'Looks like you been slaughterin' pigs, Jake.'

'Reach in that cupboard-box nailed to the wall over the bed. There's a bottle of whiskey in there.'

From beside the bed the other old man calmly said, 'Jake this one's been shot from real close.'

Caulfield said nothing until the old Rebel returned with the bottle. He was turning meat when he spoke. 'Have a drink, Simon.'

'Don't mind if I do … That's the first whiskey I've tasted in over a year. Danged bear busted my still all to hell for the mash.'

'Simon, I don't like bears. Can you patch up the still?'

'I tried but it's too broke.'

'Mine's working; you can make a batch down here if you want to.'

'That's real decent of you, Jake … Care for a drink?'

Caulfield drank, coughed, handed back the bottle and asked a question. 'Do you still trap wolves?'

'Naw … I raised two pups. It sort of spoilt me for killin' wolves, Jake.'

'Yeah, I know. I've raised a few. When a man gets to know 'em he sort of loses his idea about killin' them.'

'Jake …?'

'What.'

'How long we been neighbours?'

'Danged if I know; maybe ten, twelve years.'

'Well, most folks would think that's long enough to be snipin' at each other, wouldn't they?'

'Hand me the bottle, Simon.'

After Caulfield finished the old Confederate also had another couple of swallows. He stoppered the bottle, considered the cooking food, wanted to tell old Caulfield the meat had been cooked long enough, but kept that to himself and instead he said, 'What d'you think?'

Caulfield was busy at the stove. 'I expect you're right. Thinkin' on it, seems to me two old fellers as rickety as we is ought to sort of maybe look a little out for each other ... You want to trap wolves on my land?'

'No. I told you, I don't kill wolves any more ... Jake? Hadn't we ought to be helpin' them fellers?'

'Naw; I'll feed 'em. Besides they played hell with my house'n all ... Did you notice that feller hangin' up yonder in the new boots?'

'Yes.'

'He's my nephew.'

The old Rebel watched Caulfield turn the meat. 'Sorry to hear that, Jake.'

'Nothin' to be sorry about, Simon. He would have killed me. He was as worthless as a tanyard pup. Someday I'll tell you about him.'

Alfred Morgan appeared in the doorway. 'We're ready to bury that one, Mister Caulfield.' Morgan stepped aside as his three riders came for the corpse on the bunk. While the body was being carried out he asked the old Rebel how much he would take for his big mule.

The reaction was not quite as acerbic as it would have been if the same question had been put to Caulfield, but it came close.

'Mister, that mule ain't for sale, no matter how much money you got. If I was to sell him it wouldn't be to no cowman. I know how you fellers use your animals.'

Morgan went as far as the door before speaking again, this time to Jake Caulfield. 'We buried two, the bear's gone, we're goin' to leave now as soon as they finish with the one they just carried out.'

Caulfield turned from the stove. 'Hell, I cooked up enough for everyone.'

Morgan smiled, the fragrance of Caulfield's cooking had replaced the bear smell out where the diggers had been working. They hadn't said anything but every one of them had wrinkled their noses and rolled their eyes.

'We're obliged,' the rancher lied. 'But it'll be dark before we get well on our way. Me'n my crew is already behind at the corrals, an' them gents from Cedarton want to get back. But we're obliged for the offer anyway, Mister Caulfield.'

Old Caulfield and the former Confederate went to the doorway to watch the departure. Caulfield stepped out as Ike and Jered passed. He said, 'I'd take it kindly any time you boys is in the area ...'

They smiled, nodded, and kept riding. When they were miles on their way toward the Morgan corrals to retrieve their horses before heading home, Jered said, 'Maybe Mister Morgan wasn't right about leavin' the old man's nephew for him to bury. From what I saw of the old man he won't say a prayer or shed a tear.'

Ike was trying to fire up the broken half of his last stogie and delayed his reply until that had been accomplished. He trickled smoke, scratched inside his shirt, watched the rangeman up ahead and finally said. 'Jered, it's been a long trail, but you was right; You said we'd catch 'em an' we did, but I got to tell you, I never figured how it would end, I mean the old man, Morgan near lynchin' us for horsethieves, and that damned bear.'

Jered showed one of his rare smiles but with dusk coming no one saw it.

They reached the Morgan place. Hamilton had ridden in silence the full distance, until he veered off without speaking or waving. In the dim southerly distance a lighted lamp showed.

When Jered and Ike were saddling their own horses with Alfred Morgan assuring them they would be welcome to bed down in his bunkhouse and eat a decent meal in the morning, they declined although both were hungry and dog-tired.

They wanted to get back to town; that was their foremost thought. They left the cowmen in their yard. They waved, Morgan and his riders waved back, dusk settled, night followed, the men from Cedarton were lost in darkness when Alfred Morgan rummaged in a pocket, brought forth a golden pocket watch and held it for his riders to see. As they leaned close Morgan said, 'I'll take it over to him in a few days. I didn't want to give it to him up there; he'd have shot them as sure as we're standing here, an' I wouldn't have blamed him.'

The large, smooth-worn gold pocket watch had two names engraved on it with a brief message. 'To John Hamilton From His Loving Wife Sara Hamilton.'